GATEKEEPER'S

DAUGHTER

Eva Pohler

Published by Green Press

This book is a work of fiction. The characters, happenings, and dialogue came from the author's imagination and are not real.

THE GATEKEEPER'S DAUGHTER. Copyright 2012 by Eva Pohler.

FIRST EDITION

Book Cover Design by Keri Knutson of Alchemy Book Covers and Design.

Library of Congress Cataloging-in-Publication has been applied for

ISBN-13: 978-0615784946
ISBN-10: 0615784941

Other Books by Eva Pohler

The Gatekeeper's Sons: The Gatekeeper's Saga, Book One

The Gatekeeper's Challenge: The Gatekeeper's Saga, Book Two

The Gatekeeper's House: The Gatekeeper's Saga, Book Four

The Gatekeeper's Secret: The Gatekeeper's Saga, Book Five

The Gatekeeper's Promise: The Gatekeeper's Saga, Book Six

The Gatekeeper's Bride: A Prequel to The Gatekeeper's Saga

Hypnos: A Gatekeeper's Spin-Off, Book One

Hunting Prometheus: A Gatekeeper's Spin-Off, Book Two

Storming Olympus: A Gatekeeper's Spin-Off, Book Three

Charon's Quest: A Gatekeeper's Saga Novel

Vampire Addiction: The Vampires of Athens, Book One

Vampire Ascension: The Vampires of Athens, Book Two

Vampire Affliction: The Vampires of Athens, Book Three

The Purgatorium: The Purgatorium, Book One

Gray's Domain: The Purgatorium, Book Two

The Calibans: The Purgatorium, Book Three

The Mystery Box: A Soccer Mom's Nightmare

The Mystery Tomb: An Archaeologist's Nightmare

The Mystery Man: A College Student's Nightmare

Secrets of the Greek Revival: Mystery House #1

The Case of the Abandoned Warehouse: Mystery House #2

French Quarter Clues: Mystery House #3

Chapter One: From the Ashes

The smell of ash permeated the air, and the cry of birds echoed over the valley. Therese's mouth was dry, her lips parched. She opened her sleepy eyes, her lashes momentarily sticking together, and found her face pressed against Than's chest. The pain had finally stopped. She knew exactly where she was.

She wasn't sure how long she'd been asleep on the altar beside Than beneath the Grecian skies at the base of Mount Kronos outside of Demeter's winter cabin, but her last memory was of the pungent scent of burning flesh, and that had been replaced by the fresh smell of morning dew. Blinking her dry eyes to produce tears, she wondered at the gray papery flakes of ash covering the two of them like dirty snow, which, when she flicked it from her arm, lifted in the air and floated before drifting to the ground. She shuddered, realizing she was brushing away bits of her old self.

Than met her bewildered gaze and gave her a hesitant smile.

"You okay?" he asked.

"We're glowing. Like embers."

"Like gods." He leaned in and kissed her forehead. "My grandmother's method worked. The transformation was a success. You should see how beautiful you look." He propped himself up on his elbows, gazing lazily at her.

"What?"

He pulled a mirror from thin air and handed it to her. She gasped at her own reflection. Her eyes were brighter, her hair shinier, gleaming like the sun. Even her skin and teeth were impeccable, in spite of the flakes of ash peppering her face.

She was also much brighter than humans. Humans. It felt weird not to be included in that category anymore. And she was drop-dead gorgeous. Every one of her features was in better harmony with all the others. She looked airbrushed. Then she had this thought: "I look like my mother." She blinked her eyes several times. Tears formed but didn't fall. She was a goddess.

Her mouth dropped open. "Does this mean…?"

He smiled and nodded, a soft chuckle playing from his throat.

She jumped to her feet and brushed more of the ash from her arms, her legs. What was she wearing? The short white tunic was the only part of her not covered in the gray flakes. When she touched the silk, her dusty hand tainted it.

"I put that on you, just before you woke up," Than explained.

Blood rushed to her cheeks. Other than the locket from Athena, which had survived the flames, the tunic was the only thing on her. Did that mean he saw her naked?

The soft chuckle played from his throat once more. "Your modesty is…"

"What?" She hadn't meant that defensive edge in her voice.

"Sweet."

She relaxed a bit and smiled back at him, handing over the mirror, which immediately vanished. "I can't believe this. Am I dreaming?" She pushed off the ground and soared above Than, not quite reaching the treetops surrounding them. Disappointment quaked through her as she landed on her feet in front of the altar. "Are you a figment?"

"You're not dreaming, and I'm not a figment. That little test of yours won't work anymore, now that you can really fly."

"Now that I can…what? Are you saying I can fly?"

"You don't have very high expectations for what it means to be a god."

"I can fly? While I'm awake?" She jumped up into the air, turning somersaults just above Than's head. "I can fly! Woohoo!" Images from *Peter Pan* rushed to her, and, though she laughed at herself, she didn't stop twirling in the air.

Than shook his head. "Come back down here, you crazy girl."

She continued to turn and glide across the sky, daring to go higher, above the trees. "Whoa," she cried when she wobbled and dropped a few feet. Then, confident again, she soared up to the clouds. "Wheeee!!!" Slowly, she descended, feet first, back to the ground, but before she landed, another idea struck her. She took off running up the mountain and was halfway there in seconds. "Look how fast I can run!" Spotting a boulder wedged in the mountainside, she stopped, tugged at it, easily loosening it from the surrounding earth, and lifted it above her head. "Look how strong I am!" Her voice echoed throughout the valley.

"So I can finally kiss you without killing you, and you'd rather fly and lift heavy rocks?"

She giggled and flew to the altar and lay beside him, propping her head on an elbow. "Sorry, I'm all yours." Then, as Than's face moved near hers, she frowned.

"What's wrong?"

"Can we take a shower somewhere? We're both covered in ash." She shuddered again. Yuck. Her own dead body. She'd like to get clean of it as soon as possible.

Than snapped his fingers and a black cloud appeared above them. The cloud opened and dropped cool, refreshing rain.

"Mmm." Therese lifted her face to it and allowed it to cascade down her cheeks, neck, shoulders. "Can I do that, too? Make it rain?"

He swept her wet hair out of her eyes. "Do you really want an education on what it means to be a god? Right now?" With each word, he moved his lips nearer to hers.

"No." She looked at his mouth. "No, not really."

He reached his lips towards her, but she stopped him once again.

"Now what?"

"You burned, too. I saw you pour the kerosene all over yourself. Why?"

He cupped her chin. "I didn't want you to go through that alone."

"Wow. That's so…"

He covered her lips with his as the exhilarating rain softly washed away their ashes and reinvigorated her. She slipped her arms around his neck and pressed her body against his. He pushed her hip down onto the altar and lay half on top of her, crushing her, but she didn't mind, wanting to be as close to him as possible, making every part of her touch every part of him. She curled a leg over his and reveled at the sound of a moan escaping from his lips.

"Oh, Than. I can't believe it. We're finally together."

He snapped his fingers, and the rain stopped, and the morning sunshine warmed and dried them as they kissed, caressed, and stroked one another on Demeter's altar.

Memories of Than anointing her body—every inch of it—with ambrosia, his hands stroking her, quickly but lovingly, filled her with desire.

"Maybe we should go somewhere more private," Than whispered.

Therese nodded, but asked, nearly breathless, "What happened to your mom and grandma?"

Than stopped and sat up. "That's a good question."

Therese sat up, too. "Are you worried?"

"They gave me the vial of ambrosia. They could be in trouble."

"We need to find out."

"I've just disintegrated and dispatched to Mount Olympus to look for them."

"How do you do that?"

"Comes with the job."

"Can I do it?"

"I don't think so, but, ultimately, it'll depend on your purpose."

Just then Therese heard her aunt's voice calling to her, as though she were right there with them. "Oh my god."

"What's wrong?"

"Nothing." She tried to ignore it. "What purpose?"

He leaned back once again on his elbows. "Every god and goddess must serve humankind or the world in some way. We have to find a purpose for you, or this transformation won't last."

Therese hopped from the altar to her feet. "You never mentioned that." It seemed like pretty important information, too. "My god, how much time do I have?"

"I'm not sure, but don't worry."

She frowned, unhappy with his vague answer. She didn't think she had it in her to go through the transformation process again. The anticipation of burning to death had been horrible; the actual pain of burning alive had been worse. "I need a better answer than that. I didn't just burn to death for nothing."

"My grandmother will know. I'm looking for her, so be patient. Hephaestus just told me he hasn't seen her, but that I'm not allowed in the palace. He's going in to ask for me."

Therese heard her aunt again: "Please, Therese, wherever you are. Please come home."

She covered her face with her hands. The voice, full of desperation, seemed so close; her aunt's mouth might have been at her ear.

Than god traveled to her side. "What's wrong?"

"I didn't think about how I would be able to hear my aunt. She's talking to me, begging me to come home. How long have I been gone?"

"A few days."

Therese sat on the ground and covered her face again. "She's in full panic. I knew this would be hard—leaving her and everything—but I didn't know I would hear her crying for me. I can't bear it."

"It's worse than I thought."

Therese lifted her head. "What?"

"My mom and grandmother are being held prisoners at Mount Olympus and are awaiting trial, which we thought could happen, but..." He pulled Therese up to her feet.

"But what?"

"They're coming for us."

"Now? What'll we do?"

He shook his head.

She grabbed his hand and pointed to the top of the mountain. "Let's run and hide. Come on. There could be a cave." What was she thinking? They could go anywhere. "Let's go to China!"

"I'm disintegrated in thousands of places. There's no way I can hide. But you could."

"I'm not leaving you."

Therese wrapped her arms around his waist and pressed her cheek to his chest, the pure joy she felt moments ago vanishing. She hadn't thought completely through the consequences, and they didn't look good. His mother and grandmother were being tried in court. Her aunt and uncle were worried sick, her aunt crying out to her. And now the other gods were coming for them.

Just then roots from the ground at their feet shot up and coiled themselves around Than and Therese's legs, climbing higher and higher, cold and abrasive, ensnaring them in a net of plant. Therese screamed and Than pulled at the roots, to no avail, and soon they were encased in a kind of cocoon. Therese clung to Than, her new heart pounding, her new blood coursing through her limbs. Although she was stronger than she'd ever been in her life, it wasn't enough to break free of the trap. Then she felt the invisible plastic wrap itself around them, recognized the feeling of god travel, and the next instant, she and Than were standing in the middle of the court surrounded by the gods of Mount Olympus.

Chapter Two: Prisoners at Mount Olympus

Than could feel Therese's body trembling against him as they faced his family, the final note of Apollo's lyre lingering in the air before dead silence overtook the palace. Everyone, including his father, was there. The last time they were all together had been nearly a year ago, when Therese chose to fight McAdams, her parents' killer. Most years went by like the blink of an eye, but this past year had seemed longer than any in his life. He finally understood human longing and suffering and the dragging by of time.

Last June, while in a coma, Therese flew to him, wrapped her arms around him, and told him he was lovely. She thought she was dreaming, ignorant that she was at the junction of the dream and under worlds. In the long history of his ancient existence, no one had ever shown him such affection, and no one had made his heart race and his lips quiver with excitement like this girl, who had literally dropped from the sky.

Than needed to remind himself that his father was on his side at first. Hades had, after all, allowed Than to go to the upperworld as a mortal to try and win Therese's heart, forcing Than's brother, Hypnos, to take his place as god of the dead. In order to become a god, though, Hades required Therese to avenge her parents' murder. Therese fought valiantly on Mount Olympus against McAdams, but she refused to take his life once he was incapacitated and no longer a threat. Her compassion and her value on human life cost them their eternity together, and all the gods at Mount Olympus swore an oath on the River Styx never to make Therese a god or to retrieve her from the Underworld.

He and Therese were given another chance when Hades agreed to force Dionysus, who was not at Mount Olympus and so swore no oath, to make her a god if she could complete five challenges. Hades set her up for failure, disgusted by her decision not to kill McAdams, but when he witnessed her determination to be with Than and her cunning, strength, and bravery, somewhere along the way, Hades, too was wooed by her. Than could feel it. His father wanted Therese to succeed, even when he knew she wouldn't.

In the end, her concern for Than was her undoing. She looked back. And Than was forced to take matters into his own hands.

He was forced to break his oath.

Now, his mother and grandmother, their blond hair mussed about their lovely faces like savages, were wrapped together in a similar cocoon of roots, which was damp and possessing the rich smell of tilled earth. Hestia and Hephaestus looked away in polite sympathy, while Aphrodite stared with her hands over her mouth. Athena and Artemis looked on with skepticism, especially the latter whose forest green eyes were narrowed into an accusation. Ares wore a smirk on his red-bearded face, Hermes fear, and Apollo concern, though not as pronounced as Aphrodite's. Poseidon's eyes were on Zeus, and he looked as though he was in a hurry, impatient for this meeting to adjourn. Zeus had already told Than he would be exiled and subject to an annual visit by the maenads, so why had they been brought here?

He looked again at his mother and grandmother, their corn-blond hair pointing in all directions, their worried brown eyes meeting his. He never meant to drag them down with him. This was all wrong. Why wasn't his father helping them? He sat on his throne tugging his beard, eyes glazed like he was deep in thought.

Zeus asked for silence and then said, "Hades, you need to get your house in order. How do you propose to punish these offenders for their crimes against the rest of us?"

Hades looked up without letting go of his beard. "Well, now, it seems to me Thanatos's punishment has already been mandated by you, brother. In addition to the maenads playing havoc with his body, you've decided to exile him from Mount Olympus."

"Do you object?"

"No. The punishment is fair."

Than narrowed his eyes. Would his father do nothing to help him, then?

"But no more punishment is necessary," Hades added.

"Prevent him from marrying the girl," Ares said.

A wave of nausea overcame Than, and he bent over, holding his stomach. Therese sucked in a sharp, audible gasp. They couldn't let that happen, not after all they'd been through to be together. If it weren't for the cocoon of roots, he would punch Ares. Yes, he would very much like to punch Ares.

"No!" Aphrodite objected.

"What say you, then?" Ares quipped to the goddess of love.

"I object to these silly cocoons, first of all. Demeter and Persephone don't deserve to be treated this way. Than and Therese aren't going anywhere, besides."

The cocoons vanished, and Than felt a sense of relief to have someone stand up for him and his women.

"But something must be done," Zeus complained.

"Watching Than ripped to pieces each year is punishment enough," Hades said.

Many of the other gods and goddesses nodded their heads and muttered their agreements. Than closed his eyes for a moment, silently thanking them. Maybe his father was on his side after all.

"What of the girl?" Zeus asked.

"She fought bravely against the Hydra," Athena said. "Be merciful, father."

Than met Athena's sharp grey eyes. She liked Therese and had even given her a locket with an inscription that had helped Therese face the challenges: *The most common way people give up their power is by believing they have none.* Those words may have been more powerful than any of the gifts Therese received, including the crown of invisibility from Artemis and the traveling robe from Aphrodite.

Than pulled Therese more closely to him and asked, "Permission to speak?"

Zeus nodded.

"She committed no crime. Why should she be punished?"

"By assenting, she is guilty," Zeus replied.

Than looked around at the others present and then turned to his father, who said, "Yes, but she broke no oath and so shouldn't be subjected to the maenads."

Thank the gods for that, Than thought.

Therese shivered in his arms.

He prayed to her, "It'll be okay. You'll see." He didn't want her to know how he really felt. One never knew what to expect from the gods.

In fact, Zeus once sentenced Apollo to Tartarus for killing the Cyclops that made the thunderbolt Zeus used to strike one of Apollo's sons. The son, a demigod and not immortal, was brazen and irreverent and deserving of his punishment, but sentencing Apollo, one of the great gods, to Tartarus? That was harsh. Fortunately for Apollo, his mother stepped in and got the sentence reduced to a year of hard labor. Than could only imagine what Zeus had in store for Therese.

"Someone will need to stand in for Thanatos while he recovers," Zeus said. "That should be her punishment. No one else wants that burden."

Yet another consequence Than hadn't thought through when deciding to make Therese a god. Surely Zeus didn't expect this life-loving, inexperienced girl to handle every dead being on the planet. Plus, she had no concept of disintegration. How could she be in hundreds of thousands of places at once?

Therese's eyes widened. Than patted her back and gave her a half smile.

"That's not your call," Hades bellowed.

"But it's only fair," Hermes said. "Someone must take his place, and it won't be me."

Hades stood from his throne and moved closer to Than and Therese. "She has no experience. Knows nothing."

"Than will train her before his punishment is carried out," Zeus said.

Another lucky break, Than thought. "For how long?" he asked.

Zeus turned to the god of the Underworld. "Hades?"

"At least a week."

"Two days, then," Zeus said.

Than squeezed Therese's hand when tears flooded her eyes. "We can do this."

Her lips were close to him when she said, "I can barely look at a dead animal in the road."

He felt his throat tighten as he watched the fear darken her pretty face. He had to protect her, no matter what. The last thing he wanted was to see her suffer.

Zeus stood from his throne, spittle spraying from his brown-bearded lips as he spoke. "Furthermore, unless she fails to find a purpose and reverses her transformation, I recommend that she be forced to replace Thanatos every year during his incapacitation. No other god should be punished for a choice made by these two."

Therese's mouth fell open as she met Than's eyes. He clenched his jaw and said nothing.

"Hear, hear," the other gods said, some forlornly.

Only Hades refused his assent. Than knew his father resented being told how to run his domain. He hoped he wouldn't take his anger out on Therese.

Zeus commanded, "Take your leave, Thanatos. And you, too, Therese. Never again shall either of you set foot on Mount Olympus."

A chill moved down Than's spine.

"No!" Persephone ran to Than and circled his arm with both of hers. "Please, Zeus! Have mercy!"

"Thanatos knew the consequences," Zeus said. "He chose his path, not I."

His mother kissed his hand and then his cheek. "I know I'll see you in the Underworld, but the idea of exile from this good place forever saddens me beyond grief."

"It's okay, Mother. I rarely come here anyway. I need you to be happy for me, not sad."

She shook her head. "Oh, son. I hope you won't regret this choice you've made."

He didn't hesitate. "Never."

Chapter Three: A New Plan

Therese followed Than using god travel to his sitting room in the Underworld. Despite the cozy fire from the Phlegethon and the fireplace, she was overcome with anxiety. As if the ordeal on Mount Olympus weren't enough, her aunt was crying out to her, afraid she'd been abducted.

Therese paced the room as soon as they arrived. "I have to get a message to my family. They're worried sick!"

"What will you tell them?"

"I don't know. But I've got to tell them something. That I ran away? That would break their hearts." She continued to pace and to beat one palm with a fist.

"Tell them you took the bus to come see me. Tell them you're on your way home and you're sorry."

She flung around to face him. "You want me to lie to them? To lead them into thinking I'm coming home? That would kill them!"

"No."

"Than, what are you saying? You want me to leave you?" Her stomach felt sick.

"No. God, Therese. Would you calm down?" He tried to take her hands, but she pulled them away.

"Calm down? Calm down?" Everything was crumbling to pieces before her eyes, and he wanted her to calm down?

"Listen to me, please? Will you sit down?" He pointed to one of two leather club chairs in front of the fireplace.

She sat, but on the edge of her seat on top of her hands, clenched in tight balls beneath her thighs. She wanted to kick something. To punch something. She'd never felt this anxious. Hearing her aunt's suffering was too much. How did the gods do it?

He sat across from her, his hands on her knees. "You'll call her on the phone. You'll tell her you were upset about Vicki and wanted to see me, but you knew she and your uncle would say no. You'll tell her how sorry you are that you worried them, but you're coming home in a few days by bus and should arrive in a week's time."

"They'll insist I come home immediately." Her fingers curled around the locket from Athena. Even as a god, she felt powerless.

"Tell them you can't."

"I suppose I can say my ticket is non-refundable or something." She pulled at her fingers and jumped to her feet to pace some more. "I don't want to leave you right after, you know. I want to be here for you."

"We'll have eternity together. This way you can ease their minds."

"And tell them what? That I'm leaving again?" She fell into the club chair and put her face in her hands.

"What if..."

She looked up at him. "What? Just say it."

"What if you tell them you want to marry me?"

"They won't go for that. I'm only sixteen."

He gave her a hurt look. "You do want to though."

"Yes. Eventually. After I..." She was about to say after she graduated, but was that really necessary anymore? She was a god, for crying out loud. What was she thinking?

"After what?"

"I was going to say after I graduate high school, but I guess that's not important anymore."

"Wait. No. That's a good idea." He jumped to his feet and paced around as she had done moments before.

"What are you talking about?"

"After I'm recovered, go back to your family, in mortal form. Go back to school and graduate."

"But I'm only a junior."

"Can't you finish early?"

"If I go to summer school."

"Well?"

"Well, it might be too late. The last session starts in August. I don't know if I can still register. And I'm not sure how many classes I'd have to take. I need to talk to a counselor."

"So? Talk to one."

"Why does it matter? I don't need a high school diploma to be a god."

"No, but if you graduate, your aunt and uncle will be less likely to object to our marriage. Don't you want their blessing?"

Yes. The idea of leaving them in a state of pain—either because they'd think she was dead or that she'd run away—had burdened her from the beginning. If she could make them think she'd left them to get married, and if she could win their blessing, they wouldn't have to suffer. She stood from her chair, feeling hopeful as she bit on her lower lip.

Than put his hands on her shoulders. "Problem solved?"

"If I can graduate early. And even if I can, it means being away from you for almost a year. If I can't, it'll be two years."

"We're gods. I can visit you every day. We don't have to worry about my presence killing you."

"Really?"

"Really." He moved closer to her, so their faces were inches apart.

"Every day?"

"Every day." He leaned in and kissed her.

16

"Oh, Than!" More tears pricked her eyes. She couldn't get enough of him and didn't want to leave, ever. But her happiness wasn't the only thing important to her. "So how do we call my aunt and uncle?"

He handed her a cell phone.

"A cell phone? Really? Don't tell me you get reception down here." She half-laughed, sniffling at the same time.

"It's magic but works like one of yours. Try it."

Her hands trembled as she punched in her home number. "They're going to kill me," she whispered nervously.

Than smiled at her, his eyes mocking. "Like that's possible."

"It's an expression. Wait. Shh." How strange. She could sense her aunt answering the phone before she answered it. Now she could see her, too, standing in the kitchen, elbows on the granite bar, a hand rubbing her forehead, her straight red hair in a ponytail.

"Hello?"

"Carol, it's me."

"Therese? My God! Where are you? What happened? Are you alright?"

Therese could see Carol stand upright and turn to Richard, who was sitting on the sofa with black rings beneath dark, bloodshot eyes, but who now stood, too, his mouth agape.

"I, I'm okay."

"Thank God! Where are you? What's going on?"

"I was upset. About Vicki. I wanted to see Than. But I'm coming back. I'm sorry I didn't tell you. I was afraid you'd say no."

"My God, Therese. Do you know what we've been through the past three days? Three days! You should have called before now. The police are…"

"The police? You called the police?"

17

"Of course we called the police. What did you think we'd do? You disappeared. We thought you were stolen."

Therese could see her aunt sink into Richard's arms. He led her to the sofa, and they both collapsed into it.

"You better call Jen, too."

"I'm so sorry."

"Where are you?"

"At Than's. But I'm taking the bus home in a few days. I'll be home in a week, I think."

"A week? You get on that bus today, Therese. Do you hear me?"

"I can't. The return ticket is nonrefundable."

"I'll buy you a new one. Better yet, I'll fly down and get you."

"No. Please. I need time."

"You and Than haven't…"

"What?"

"Are you being safe?"

"Oh my God! Nothing to worry about. I just needed to see him."

Yuck. Her aunt was asking about sex?

"Does he live with his parents or alone?"

"His parents."

"And they're there?"

Therese looked up at Than. "Yes. They're here. Well, his dad is. His mom's, um, visiting his grandmother."

"Let me speak to his dad."

"You can't. He's working right now."

"Call me tonight, when his father returns, so I can speak with him, and call me every night till you're home safe, to let me know you're still okay."

"Okay."

"You promise?"

18

"I promise."

"I still can't believe you did this to me."

"I'm so sorry."

As she hung up the phone, she closed her eyes and sighed, wondering if her aunt and uncle would ever forgive her. Then her stomach balled up in a knot at the thought of having to ask Hades to talk to her aunt.

Than kissed the top of her head. She wrapped her arms around his neck and relished his comforting squeeze. "We'll get through this," he said.

She nodded, pulling back and brushing tears from her cheeks. They felt different. Less wet. Almost as though her cheeks were numb.

Next she called Jen. As she punched in the number, she could see Jen with her bright blond hair in two braids in the barn talking to a girl their age she'd never met before. The girl was shorter than Jen with long brown hair and a thin frame. Jen answered the phone in the barn.

"It's me," Therese said.

Jen stopped, rigid. "Are you okay? Where are you?"

"With Than. I'm coming home. I just freaked, you know? I'm sorry I scared everyone."

"Have you called your aunt?"

"Yeah."

"Why didn't you tell me? I could have kept your secret and come up with a cover so your aunt and Pete and everybody wouldn't go all nutso."

"Pete?"

"When will you be back?"

"In a week or so. I'm taking the bus."

"Call me or text me, okay?"

"I will. Who's that with you?"

"What? How did you know someone was with me?" Jen glanced in all directions, as though searching for Therese.

"I thought I heard another voice."

"That's weird. She didn't say anything. Anyway, it's Vicki's cousin, Courtney."

"Vicki's cousin?"

"Yeah. She and her mom are visiting Mr. Stern for the rest of the summer. Her mom is Mr. Stern's sister."

"I didn't know he had a sister. That's good." Therese was glad for Vicki's dad. She'd been worried about him being alone after Vicki died, only a year after her mother took her life. Hopefully having family around for the summer would ease his pain.

"Yeah. He called your aunt and my mom to see if we'd spend some time with Courtney, so she wouldn't get bored. Turns out she knows a lot about horses. Her mom grew up around them. They're from...hang on, did you say North Carolina?"

"North Dakota," the girl named Courtney corrected.

"North Dakota," Jen said into the phone.

"Cool. I'm looking forward to meeting her." Therese felt slightly jealous that Jen was having fun with a friend. She hadn't seemed all that worried about Therese's disappearance. "Later, Jen."

When she hung up, she internally reprimanded herself for thinking that way.

"What's wrong?" Than asked.

"Nothing. I'm an idiot, that's all."

Than looked back at her, his mood suddenly dark.

"What?" she asked.

"You regret..."

20

"No. Absolutely not. How can you think that? No. I have no regrets." She hugged him, feeling his mood lighten and his body relax. Then she added, "Things are a mess, though. I need to fix them."

"First things first." He touched the tip of her nose and brushed a stray tear from her cheek. "I have to train you."

Chapter Four: Goddess of Death in Training

Of all the places Than had to be today, this death seemed the gentlest for Therese's first time. He didn't want to throw her in the middle of a tough one. He needed to help her gradually get used to people dying all around them.

Therese stood beside him in a hospital room near the bed of an old woman, whose eyes were closed, breathing erratic. Two middle-aged women sat on either side of the old one, holding her hands and praying. Therese said, without speaking, "I can hear them."

"Please let her go easy," one prayed.

"Take Mama to heaven," the other prayed.

"She's almost ready." Than wrinkled his nose at the pungent smells of urine, perspiration, and body odor, not uncommon in his line of work, but desensitized he was not. "When her body stops, you have to reach in and put your hand on her soul. She won't know what to do. We'll guide her, okay?"

Therese nodded, looking apprehensive but determined. That's what he loved most about her: her determination.

"Say hi to Daddy," one of the women said, sensing the end. "Tell him we love him!"

In the next instant, the old woman's eyes flashed open, and she looked directly at Therese. Her mouth opened wide, and she gasped.

"Can she see us?"

"Yes. Tell her it's okay."

"It's okay, Madeline. I'm here to help." She looked at Than. "How do I know her name?"

"It's like that with everyone. You'll see."

The old woman collapsed against her pillow, her eyes fixed and unblinking. Her breathing stopped.

"Mama?"

"She's gone! Call the nurse!"

Than led Therese closer to the bed. "Now reach in, just at her shoulders."

"Into her body?"

Than took Therese's hand, and together they penetrated the old woman's shoulders and fell upon the airy, feathery feel of something not quite solid, but palpable.

"Help her out."

Together they helped the soul emerge from the woman's body and out into the room.

"It's going to be okay, Madeline," Than said to the woman. He kept a hand on her shoulder.

Therese did the same, and together they left the bustle of nurses, machines, and departed loved ones to god travel with the woman to the banks of the Acheron where Charon waited on his raft. As they neared Cerberus, Therese gave the three-headed dog a friendly wave, and he wagged his dragon tail as his three tongues hung from his three mouths. Cerberus loved her almost as much as Than did.

They passed Cerberus and entered the iron gate. Then Charon delivered them to the judges, who declared the woman destined to the Fields of Elysium. Once they saw her safely there, Therese and Than returned to his rooms.

Therese sank into the leather club chair by the fire. "That wasn't so bad." Although she was a bit drained looking, something in her eyes appeared radiant, triumphant even. "I didn't think I could handle it, but I could. It felt good. Like I was helping."

"Yes. Those are the best cases—when they're ready to go and their loved ones have accepted it."

"I guess most cases aren't so easy, huh?"

Than shook his head. She had so much more in store, so much pain and agony. He wished he hadn't put her in this position. He wished he could spare her from it all. Her willingness to suffer for him made him love her all the more.

"I keep telling myself it's temporary—their pain and sadness, I mean."

"That's right. That's a good girl." He leaned in and kissed her cheek. "Ready?"

"Already?"

Than frowned. "This job is never-ending. That's your first big lesson. Remember, I'm all over the world right now. You'll have to be, too."

He helped her from the chair and into his arms. "Hold me close," he whispered. "This won't be easy."

She gave him a brave smile, which made him proud. "By the way," he said. "Demeter says you have three months to find your purpose."

"Three months?" He watched her count on her fingers. She was so cute. "October. What's today?"

"July third in some places. The fourth in others."

"October third. I have to figure this out by October third."

The room was small and stuffy, the stringent smell of anesthetic and cleaner overpowering the lesser one of urine. The thirty-six year-old woman, bald and sallow, lay in a morphine-induced sleep in a hospice bed with her older brother collapsed and sleeping in a nearby chair in the dim circle of light from a bedside lamp. The dying woman's six-year-old twin sons and eleven-year-old daughter had already said their goodbyes the night before. Her ex-husband and his new wife and children had also come and gone. The only one left was her lifelong friend, her brother, and, knowing her time was close, he had refused to leave her side. Than usually took it upon himself to wake such a dedicated loved one just before or after the body expired so the soul could whisper goodbye in passing.

Therese held his hand with a tight grip. He could hear her thoughts, aimed at him, "Poor woman! Poor woman! She's so young, her children not ready. This doesn't seem fair."

"Life isn't fair," came his automatic reply. He wished he didn't have to put Therese through this.

"I can feel how hard she fought," Therese said. "And I can sense the pain she was in before the medication took over. The cancer started in her breasts but spread throughout her body. I can feel it in her liver and in her kidneys. It's eating her alive from the inside."

Than gave her a solemn nod. "We're here to end her pain."

"But her children."

"They have their father and a stepmother who love them. Not all left behind are as fortunate."

"Fortunate?"

"Sorry. Poor choice of words."

"I can feel her dying," Therese said. "I feel it all around my body, especially my chest. It's weird how I can sense her every breath, her every movement."

"It's time to reach inside for her soul. I'll just nudge her brother awake."

"Why not let him sleep?"

"He'll feel good tomorrow knowing he had the chance to say goodbye."

Therese gave him a loving smile that made his heart fill up with joy even in the midst of this overwhelming sadness. Together they reached into the woman's body for that feathery part of her still alive.

"This way, Tamara," Than said.

Her brother opened his eyes and looked at her, instantly aware that she was no longer breathing. He grabbed her hand. "Sis?"

The brother seemed to look directly at his sister's soul, as though he could see it. "I love you," he said. "Wait for me."

Tamara was at first confused, but when she heard her brother's words, she turned and touched his face. "I love you, too."

Then Therese and Than swept her off to the banks of the Acheron and onto Charon's raft. After they left her in the Elysian Fields, they returned to Than's room so Therese could collect herself. She was trembling, her cheeks wet with tears.

"This isn't easy," she whispered.

"No," he said. "No, it's not." He took her in his arms and held her. "It gets much worse." He kissed her wet lips tenderly and looked into her eyes. "Ready?"

She held him tightly for many seconds. Then she wiped her eyes and cheeks and gave him a brave nod. He could not be more proud.

Chapter Five: The Trapped Boy

Therese stood beside Than near a mountain of rubble and debris where hundreds of people in various uniforms and civilian clothing, of multiple nationalities and ethnicities, dug with shovels and combed the site with metal detectors and, unfortunately, carried bodies, most of them dead, off to the nearby ambulances awaiting them.

Other people—old men and women and children—huddled along the perimeter, weeping and praying. Some of their prayers, she could hear.

"Let my grandson be alive."

"Help the rescue workers find my baby boy."

The prayers weren't in English, but Therese could understand them. Adding to their anxiety was the fact that dusk was settling, and darkness wouldn't be far behind. As she looked over the scene, she felt a pang of sorrow for Than, whose entire existence was filled with scenes exactly like it. More than ever, she wanted to add joy to his life. She wondered if her love for him could be enough to tip the scales of the balance of his life toward happiness.

"Where are we?" she asked Than.

"In a Turkish town near the border of Iran. These are earthquake victims. A building, several stories high, collapsed earlier in the week. I've taken over two hundred souls to the Underworld. Men, women, and children of all ages. This was a building of department stores among other businesses."

"Oh my god." She covered her mouth.

"There's one more boy here about to die. It won't be easy, so brace yourself. He's young, only four years old, and has been trapped beneath this rubble for five days. The others trapped with him have already died. He's the last of them."

Tears rushed to Therese's eyes. "Okay. I'm ready."

Now she could hear the prayers of the boy. "I want my mother and grandmother. I want my mother and grandmother." Over and over, his prayer was the same. She could sense his desperate thirst and hunger, but his only prayer was for his mother and grandmother. "Ahn-neh! Ba-ba-ahn-neh!"

"How do you do this every day, all day?" she asked as they stepped closer to the rubble above the boy.

"You're about to find out."

"But you do it all the time, forever. How do you avoid depression?"

"Until I met you, I was depressed—mainly because my life never varied. But look around you."

"What do you mean?"

"See how they all work together, helping one another?"

Therese surveyed the multitudes digging, sweeping, praying, carting, reviving. "It *is* heartwarming to see people working in harmony for a common cause." She held her eyes on Than for a moment longer, realizing the thing she loved most about him: He always managed to see the good in things and to make the most out of each circumstance.

"Some of them are enemies, but to save the victims, they put aside their differences." He took her hand. "It's almost time for the boy. Let's go to him."

She squeezed his hand and nodded. He softly kissed her forehead.

Therese cringed as they passed lifeless bodies. Some of their eyes and mouths were still open; they died gasping for their last breaths. Others were crushed and had likely died instantly. All were covered in dirt. The boy, Sahin, cried dry tears and muttered soundless words: "Ahn-neh! Ba-ba-ahn-neh!" His hair was white with powdered concrete. Rings of caked mud circled each eye where pre-hydration tears must have gathered on his light brown skin. His brows were knitted together, his eyes half closed with fatigue and dread. He sat on the ground with his knees pressed against his growling stomach, all but his head hidden in the wedge between two collapsed walls. His parched lips moved their soundless cries. "Ahn-neh! Ba-ba-ahn-neh!"

"Can you see me?" Therese asked the boy.

The boy nodded, sucking in his lips, and for a moment his prayers halted.

"I'm here to help you," Therese added. "Are you in pain?"

He said the words for thirsty and scared. Then he continued his chant of "Ahn-neh! Ba-ba-ahn-neh!"

Therese glanced at Than, wishing the boy's torment would end. How much longer did they have to wait?

Clutched in Sahin's hand was a yellow toy the size of his fist. He held it out to her, above the block of cement trapping the rest of his body, so she took it. It was a miniature dump truck.

"For Mother," he whispered in his language. "Please give it to her."

Above their heads, a thick concrete beam lay across other broken walls, creating a small space that allowed air to circulate. This had surely kept the boy alive. Otherwise, he would have expired days ago with the others. Therese could sense the rescue workers above them, digging the rubble on top of the beam overhead. They were so close. She wished she could hasten their work and help them find the boy, but she knew she wasn't to interfere. Than had told her again and again it was not his place; nor was it hers. The earth could not support a human population that never died. But she wished people didn't have to die so young and in such tragic ways, with their mothers and grandmothers praying for their lives.

She wished all people could live to old age and then die a peaceful death. Why did things have to be this way? Now that she was a god, could she change them?

Maybe that could be her purpose—her service to humankind. She could be the goddess of those too young to die. She could save people from dying before old age.

Than knew her thoughts before she spoke them. She hadn't realized she'd been sharing them with him this entire time.

"We tried that once before," he said. "It was a terrible time in human history. We thought we were adding value to human life, but we were actually diminishing it."

"What happened?"

"People stopped caring."

She looked up again toward the sound of digging and scraping. They were so close! "So there's nothing we can do to save this boy?" she asked.

The boy looked at her as though he could hear and understand her. "Ahn-neh! Ba-ba-ahn-neh!" He pressed his little legs against the concrete wall for what must have been the hundredth time. He squirmed against his trap, like a butterfly in a jar.

Therese held out her hand to comfort him. "I'll give your toy to your mother. I promise."

The multitude of prayers above them was overwhelming, but even louder were the fervent sounds of digging and scraping. The rescuers were closer, about to break through. They would miss the boy by minutes!

The boy lifted his now empty hand above his concrete trap and circled his fingers around Therese's index finger. He looked at her as though he knew it was time. She gave him a sad smile and kissed his little hand, which seemed to hasten his death. But just as his eyes widened and he sucked in what should have been his last breath, a shovel struck through the rubble above, and a hand reached down and grabbed the boy by his arm.

Sahin flew up from his trap and into the hands of a rescue worker. A storm of activity followed. Therese and Than left the heap to watch as the boy was rushed, oxygen mask to his face, across the debris to an ambulance. The mother and grandmother lifted their faces as though they knew who he was before seeing the child's face. Other parents, too, looked on with hope.

"What just happened?" Therese asked Than, full of excitement. "I could feel him die. I could sense his death with my whole being, like a pressure, like god travel. My heart knew he was dead one instant, but then he was alive the next. Does that happen often? Is he going to live?"

"Hold on." Than took her hand and together they returned the toy dump truck to the boy's hand. "You can give this to your mother," Than whispered just before he and Therese left the back of the ambulance and the doors were closed and the engine roared to life.

He took Therese to his sitting room and held her on his lap. "Someone intervened." He ran a hand through his hair. "It was Athena. Only gods of Mount Olympus can, and they do so rarely. Someone must have moved her with their prayers. Perhaps a soldier, since she is their special patron."

Therese buried her face in Than's neck. She was happy for the boy and his family, but sad for all the others who, for whatever reason, had not moved Athena. She held back her tears, though, and gritted her teeth, because she had to be strong for Than. This was only the beginning of her training, and she had to make him feel secure about leaving his duties in her hands. She was death, and death, though sad for those left behind, was a gift to those who suffered and was inevitable to all.

Than's strong arms wrapped more tightly around her, and a sigh escaped her lips. She peeked up at his hooded eyes, his bottom lip

31

between his teeth. The sight of his beauty, so close to her, made her shiver. Despite the gloomy training, she was grateful to be with him.

She bent her face to his and said, "So what's next?"

He pushed a strand of hair behind her ear. "You need to learn to disintegrate."

"Yeah, what exactly is that, anyway?" She shifted in his lap so she could better face him. "I mean, how does it work?"

He bit his lower lip, drawing her attention to his mouth again. She couldn't believe she was really here with him, and she wasn't ready to give him up to the maenads. Two days wasn't long enough. She suddenly felt giddy after all the depressing events.

"Let me see if I can think of an analogy," he said.

As he gazed up at the shadows on the ceiling of his room, she couldn't resist taking a quick nibble of his lower lip.

He squeezed each of her upper arms, laughing. "Holy moly."

"Holy moly? Who says that anymore? Holy moly!"

"At one time it was a very popular expression." He tickled her sides. "Now quit making fun of me and pay attention."

"Yes, sir." She smirked.

He tickled her again.

"Stop! Stop and tell me your analogy."

"Okay. Imagine a shower head."

She pulled her head back and bent her brows. "A shower head? Okay?"

"Dozens of individual streams pour through the openings of the shower head, and all of those streams are water—not part water, but fully, wholly H20, correct?"

"Correct."

"Both the overall flow coming from the shower head and the independent streams consist of one hundred percent water."

"Correct."

"And yet the streams are all part of the flow of water even as they are complete in and of themselves."

"What a philosopher you are." She playfully punched his arm.

"That's disintegration. You are one hundred percent you, but you are simultaneously in many places, and in each place you occupy, you are still one hundred percent you."

"I think I get it. Piece of cake. Let's do this thing."

"But it can be overwhelming, processing all the stimuli. Because even as you disintegrate into multiple selves, each self knows what every other self is experiencing. You are inundated with sights, sounds, smells, etc."

She jumped from his lap. "Well, I'm as ready as I'll ever be. Beam me up, Scotty."

He laughed. "That saying's almost as old as holy moly."

"I don't think so."

"Let's see…of the two of us, who's been around longer?"

"Oh, shut up."

"So, here we go. We'll stay here, in my room, but we'll also go see Hip in the field of poppies, okay?"

"Okay."

"Ready?"

"Ready."

For a moment she thought it was interesting he'd used water to describe disintegration, because she felt, at that instant, as though water— cold water—was running across her back. She even reached over her shoulder, half expecting to find herself wet. She now had four arms and two backs, and her peripheral vision was like looking through a kaleidoscope at a bunch of distorted, but patterned, images. When Than spoke, she heard an echo, as though he used a microphone and loudspeaker.

"Are-are-you-you-okay-okay?"

Slowly, like when you can hear an echo of yourself on your cell phone, she said, "I-feel-dizzy."

"I-I-want-want-one-one-of-of-you-you-to-to-sleep-sleep-and-and-the-the-other-other-of-of-you-you-to-to-stay-stay-awake-awake."

"Hu-uh?"

He pulled her onto his lap in one of the club chairs in front of the fireplace, and, simultaneously, led her across the field of poppy. She felt sleepy and wanted to lie down.

"Over-over-here-here."

They lay together among the flowers, and she closed her eyes, but she could still see him, holding her in the club chair, leaning in for a kiss. Hip appeared, and she was simultaneously kissing Than and trying to hear what Hip had to say. She couldn't understand a word.

"What?"

"You look like you've been drinking," Hip repeated.

"I'm dizzy and confused."

"Well, what I was trying to tell you is that I think I'm in love with your friend Jen."

"You stay away from her."

He put his hands on his slim hips. "Just because you're a god now doesn't mean you get to tell me what to do. Besides, she needs me."

"She doesn't need you."

"She's heartbroken, and I make her feel better."

"What do you mean she's heartbroken?"

"Some friend you are. Didn't you know Matthew broke up with her?"

34

Therese realized she was hovering above the poppies, above where her body slept. Than was beside her. She glared at Hip. "How do you know they broke up?"

"At night, she begs me to come, to help her forget. She calls me Mr. Sandman."

Therese muttered the familiar lyric, "Mr. Sandman, bring me a dream."

"Exactly. I've been comforting her for three days now."

Therese turned to Than. "Matthew must have broken up with her the day I left to face the hydra. She didn't say anything to me on the phone."

Than put an arm around her. "She'll be okay."

"She needs me. Hip's right. I haven't been a very good friend."

"Courtney's with her."

Therese's stomach felt sick. Courtney. Would Courtney replace her as Jen's new best friend? She should be glad that Jen wouldn't be alone when Therese left to live in the Underworld, but she wasn't. Even when Courtney returned to North Dakota, they could email and text. The thought of it made her sad and hurt. Could she email and text from the Underworld?

"And after that we'll try a dozen," Than said.

"Yes. Three, six, twelve. That's a good plan," Therese said, suddenly aware that she'd been having two conversations simultaneously, and was able to follow both.

"You're doing good," Than said. "I'm sorry about Jen."

She and Than hung out in the dream world with Hip, lounged on the club chairs and made out, and disintegrated once more, dispatching to Tartarus to visit Tizzie.

"Hey." Tizzie, her dark, serpentine curls hiding her face, spoke without looking up from the soul she tortured, a young man whom

Therese sensed had been there a few years. He lay on a marble slab bound at the wrists and ankles to leather straps connected to chains on a pulley. Tizzie cranked the pulley, which pulled at the straps and stretched the soul.

"Can souls feel pain?" Therese asked, sensing this one could.

"It's more psychological than physical," Tizze said. "But, yes."

The soul looked at them warily, tears slipping from the corners of his transparent eyes.

"You do realize the oath-breakers are brought here while their bodies heal?" Tizzie's black, serpentine curls momentarily parted as she looked up from her victim. The emerald choker around her neck and the silver halter top gleamed with the light cast by the Phlegethon. Her wolf paced a few yards away, ready to serve her.

"Are you going to stretch me as well?" Than asked.

Tizzie glanced up at the jug carriers, drenched from their leaking vessels as they walked across a narrow bridge above the bottomless pit. "I may require you to fill a bath to wash away your sins, like those women."

"But their jugs are leaking faster than they can carry them," Therese noted.

"Exactly."

"Or should I help poor Sisyphus by taking over his rock?" Than offered.

Tizzie abruptly turned to face them, her eyes dripping with blood. "You can't take over the punishment of another."

"Relax, I was only joking."

Tizzie's eyes returned to their usual black discs. "You deserve no additional punishment, brother. You have a kind heart, and the maenads are punishment enough."

"So what will you have me do? Twiddle my thumbs?"

"You won't be here long."

"If Apollo…"

"He won't touch you, I don't think. Not with Ares against it."

"In that case," Than said. "I've seen gods require days, weeks to heal."

"You can take over my job while I take a holiday in Paris."

"Oh, yay," Than said with sarcasm. "Can't wait."

"So why are you really here, if it's not to admire my work?"

"Therese is practicing disintegration. We're in two other places together. We're going to watch you for a while, if that's okay, while we disintegrate and dispatch to other locations to retrieve the dead."

"Watch away. Let's see how far I can stretch him before he breaks."

Chapter Six: Time's Up

Than couldn't stop laughing. In the presence of the dead, he was somber and melancholy, and he was making sure Therese could handle each horrific scene they visited, but here in his room in front of the fireplace with Therese in his lap, he was having the time of his life. He was testing her ability to concentrate on her duties in other places while he distracted her here.

And he was enjoying the hell out of his distraction techniques.

The brightness of her green eyes framed by her long, dark lashes undid him every time she looked at him. There was something in her expression, too. Even if he hadn't been able to hear her prayers of love and longing, her sweet eyes said it all. He wondered if his eyes held the same message for her.

"Yes." She touched her forehead to his. "They do."

Had he directed those thoughts to her? Had he been praying to her?

"I guess so. If I can hear them." She looked at his mouth. "Now where were we?"

"Here." He kissed her neck. He'd been kissing every inch of her skin, starting with her forehead and working his way around her face.

She moaned as his lips worked their way down from below her chin, behind her ear, and to her throat. "Oh my."

Now he followed a shoulder and kissed down the length of her smooth, soft arm. "Put your hand on Melvin's shoulder, Therese. Stay aware in all locations."

She closed her eyes. "Oh my heaven. Don't stop."

He sucked each of her fingers.

"Patricia's going to miss the raft if you don't keep her steady."

"Sweet heaven. I've got her. Don't stop."

He laughed. "I'm going to make this even more interesting."

Her eyes shot open and she gave him a playful grin. "How?"

"Let's disintegrate and dispatch to Demeter's winter cabin. We can make out there while we make out here." He leaned in and licked her bottom lip before smiling and adding, "That is, if you think you can handle it."

"Where's Demeter?"

"Mount Olympus. The cabin's empty."

She tucked in her chin and looked up at him through her dark lashes. "Bring it on."

They disintegrated and landed with a thud on the bed in his grandmother's guest bedroom. For a moment, he worried he'd crushed her, but her laughter told him otherwise.

"I hit my head!"

"Oops. Sorry." He shifted his weight so he wasn't fully on top of her.

He broke out in laughter again when he felt her arms at his torso tugging him back on. "I'm a god now, remember? You can't hurt me that easily."

He climbed back on.

"Wait."

He met her eyes, which looked full of mischief. They were beautiful.

"This isn't sacrilegious is it? Making out here and in your room while we're escorting souls to the underworld?"

"It's good practice for you," he insisted. "It's important."

"Important."

"Necessary."

"Necessary." She gave him a smile that showed she didn't quite believe him.

"Now, back to your lessons." He ran his mouth along her jawline.

"In that case, do what you're doing back in your room. The same thing, but in the other ear. I want to see how that feels."

He liked the way she was thinking and moved his mouth to her ear.

She gasped and whispered, "Oh. My. God."

Just then the door crashed open, and Than immediately sensed the presence of two gods—Hermes and Dionysus. He and Therese flew to their feet, holding one another as they faced the two intruders.

"What the hell do you want, cousins?" Than asked.

"Sorry to be the one to tell you," Hermes said. "But it's time."

"Zeus said two days!" Therese moved her body in front of Than.

Dionysus stepped toward her and twirled a strand of her hair between his fingers. His own golden hair hung in the same two long braids at the back of his head Than remembered from their last encounter, and his half-naked body gleamed in the sunlight pouring in from the windows. "That may well be, but Zeus has apparently changed his mind."

Than pulled Therese into his arms and away from the clutches of Dionysus.

She searched Than's face, her brows nearly touching. "Can he do that?"

Than held her face in his hands and forcefully pressed his lips to hers. "I love you. Remember that. Now go and do your duty in my place."

"But I'm not ready. I haven't even disintegrated to more than twenty places. How can I manage hundreds of thousands?"

"Thanatos has no choice but to go with us," Dionysus said grimly.

"Sorry, Therese," Hermes added. "But you'll get the hang of it. And Than will be back to himself soon."

Than's throat constricted as he anticipated the pain he was about to endure. He recalled the sharp sting of his thumb being ripped from his hand and shuddered. "It won't be long. I promise."

"No! Don't take him! He doesn't deserve this!" She turned to Dionysus, and for a moment Than thought her eyes would bleed like the eyes of his sisters. "This is your fault! If you'd only helped us, he wouldn't have had to break his oath!"

"So I forced him to go against his word?" the god of the vine mocked.

"You selfish bastard! You could have helped us!" Therese beat at the god of wine's chest.

Than's mouth dropped open at Therese's choice of words, and he held her back, back in his arms. Dionysus was a bastard, in all its connotations, and the fact that he had a chip on his shoulder and hated all the other gods for his isolation meant he probably didn't appreciate being reminded of it.

Dionysus narrowed his eyes. "I'm going to enjoy this now, thanks to you, missy! I'll be sure to instruct the maenads to take their time."

Therese turned her wide eyes to Than. "What have I done?"

Before Than could stop her, Therese threw herself on the ground, prostrate before the wine god. "I beg you with all my heart to forgive me. I'm your servant. If there's any way you can minimize Than's pain and suffering, I'll be your servant for all eternity."

"Therese!" Than cried, his blood rushing to his face in a pool of heat. "You don't know what you're doing! You can't swear yourself to him and live a life with me." He plucked her from the ground and turned her to face him. "What are you saying? You'll be with him?"

Her face flushed now, too. "No. That's not what I meant."

"That's how he'll take it."

Therese glanced at the golden braids, the tan face. Than hated that he wore only the loin cloth. Exhibitionist bastard.

"I only meant I'd do his bidding, any time he needed help."

"When a woman says that to a man…" Than couldn't finish.

Dionysus and Hermes were overcome with laughter. Than gritted his teeth.

Before Than could speak, Hermes put a hand on his shoulder and said, "Sorry, ol' cousin. Truly. But you should see the looks on each of your faces." He busted out in laughter again.

Dionysus clapped a hand against Than's back. "No worries, Thanatos. My heart belongs to Ariadne."

Nevertheless, Than noticed the once over Dionysus gave Therese.

"She is tempting though."

Than pulled back his fist, ready to launch it at Dionysus, but Hermes and Therese held him back.

Dionysus laughed again.

Hermes grew somber, running a hand through his curly black hair. "You're like a little brother to me. I hate to do this."

Roots shot up from the ground and curled themselves around Than's ankles, legs, and body as they'd done less than twenty-four hours ago when he and Therese had been taken to Mount Olympus.

"Touch my hand," he said to Therese. "It's time for you to take over."

Her fingers trembled when she reached through the web of roots and put her hand in his. He hoped and prayed to all the gods that Therese could manage without him.

"Don't worry," she said bravely. "I've got this. And I'm coming with you."

"No. I don't want you to."

42

"How can I not?"

"I don't want you to see me suffer."

"I have to be there for you. I can't let you go through it alone."

He didn't want to tell her what he was really thinking: he was embarrassed by the thought of how he would behave. Would he cry and scream like a baby? He didn't want her to see him like that.

"You need to concentrate on your duty."

"My duty is first and foremost to you."

She reached her pretty face in through the webbing and kissed him once more. She kissed him like a mortal saying goodbye, as though she didn't really believe he'd be back.

Chapter Seven: The Maenads

Therese was instantly overwhelmed by the souls from all over the world calling to her. She disintegrated thousands of times and dispatched to all walks of life. Despite her initial disorientation, she resolved to regain focus, finding that if she used her instinct more than her mind, she could work more efficiently. She went with the natural flow of it, trying not to think, but to stay in the zone like a seasoned athlete, letting her body—bodies—do the work.

But one of her remained with Than as they god traveled from Demeter's winter cabin with Hermes and Dionysus to a pine forest on Mount Kithairon. She chewed ferociously at the inside of her lips as sweat beaded on her face. If only she had succeeded in the fifth challenge. She wished she could trade places with Than. Maybe she could.

As she followed the gods up the hill toward a large throng of dancers and music makers, she cried, "Wait!" Her voice echoed through the valley. She'd forgotten how powerful she was now that she, too, was a god.

The other gods stopped and turned. Even the music stopped in the distance.

"This isn't fair!" She clenched her fists at them. "Than had no choice but to take that oath. He was forced into it. It shouldn't count."

"You should have made your case at Mount Olympus," Dionysus said. "It's too late now." He and the others turned to go on, up the hill.

"Can't I take his place?"

They stopped to look back at her again.

"What are you talking about, Therese?" Than snapped.

"Didn't Admetus once get his wife to take his place in the Underworld? Can't we ask for a similar deal?"

"No!" Than practically burst from his webbing as he ripped and snarled at her like a caged animal. "Stop this! Are you mad?"

"I could look into it," Hermes said.

"I won't allow it!" Than growled. "Now stop, Therese, or I swear!"

"Swear what? It's my fault! I should be the one to suffer the maenads."

Dionysus turned to Than. "You lucky rogue."

Than said between gritted teeth, "She won't be taking my place."

The god of wine grabbed Therese by the elbow too roughly for her comfort.

"What are you doing?" she asked as he pulled her closer to him. His mostly naked body unsettled her.

He looked deeply into her eyes, studying them. "You would lay at the hands of the maenads for him? Tell me the truth. Do you mean what you say?"

She glared at him. "Absolutely."

"Damn you, Dionysus!" Than growled. "Let her go! I won't let her do it!"

Dionysus ignored Than's shouts. "Has Cupid pierced your heart with one of his arrows?"

Therese shook her head. She thought of Pete.

"Can you teach me to win Ariadne's heart?"

Therese flinched with surprise. "I don't know."

"What's the secret to love?"

"Shouldn't you ask Aphrodite?"

"I'm asking you."

Therese combed her mind for the best answer, studying Than's pained expression as he struggled against the net of roots. "Sacrifice. You win someone's love by making sacrifices."

45

Dionysus pushed her away from him with disgust. "I don't believe in making sacrifices. I believe in living life to the fullest every moment of the day!"

Therese stumbled, but caught herself before she fell. She stood tall and proud, remembering that she was a god, too. "That's why you're alone."

He narrowed his eyes at her as though they were weapons.

"Let me take his place," she said again.

"No."

Before she could speak another word, he god traveled with Than to the throng of people up the mountain. She and Hermes followed close behind.

She fought against the one or two hundred women crowding around Dionysus and the cocoon of roots still encasing Than. Their bodies writhed against her, their long hair thrashing across her face. She reached through the roots and took his hand, praying that she'd remain at his side for as long as she could.

The music roared to life through the lyres and flutes of at least a dozen satyrs, and the women around her flailed their arms in the air and jerked their bodies in a state of madness as the roots slowly fell away from Than.

He turned to her with a hint of panic in his eyes. "It's okay. Do your job."

She was shoved aside as the women clamored toward Than, grabbing his limbs from all directions. Therese hoped he would expire quickly so he wouldn't suffer long.

Wait. He had said, "Do your job." Now that she was the god of death, she could take his soul any time, couldn't she? She reached into his body and pulled, but his soul would not come free. What the…?

"That only works with humans," he said through gritted teeth. He turned up toward the clouds, opened his mouth, and cried out in pain as his left arm was ripped from his torso. His scream echoed across the valley, over the sounds of the music makers. Birds scattered from the treetops. Blood spilled from his body, and the severed flesh of his arm pit hung grotesquely. It was *his* body being torn apart, but it felt like *her* heart.

Panic gripped her. "No! How long do I have to wait before I can take you?" She wrenched her fingers around the feathery, ethereal mass that was his soul, ready to take him as soon as she could pull him free. Her tears poured down her face and into her mouth and mixed with his blood.

He couldn't reply.

The maenads ripped his leg at the knee and he howled across the mountainside.

"Hermes! Help me preserve him!" she cried. She disintegrated into three more and collected Than's bloody limbs, still warm and twitching in her hands, blood running down her arms.

A hand, an arm, the other leg—as soon as they were ripped from his torso, she bounded to retrieve them, sometimes fighting off a maenad wishing to eat the flesh. Hermes helped, his face grim.

Then the maenads ripped off Than's head, and his soul came free. One of her found his precious head, closed her eyes, and cringed as she added it to the rest of her collection. She couldn't look; she just couldn't look. Another of her wrenched what was left of his torso free from the wild women and dispatched in multiples to Demeter's cabin to find Demeter and Persephone waiting with Apollo.

"Apollo?" She burst into tears, grateful to see the god of healing and traumatized by the fact that she was holding the bits of her true love. Her three fragmented selves lovingly lay Than's parts on the altar without quite looking at them, and then she fell onto the floor, shuddering and sobbing, allowing the trauma and grief to consume her.

As she led his bewildered soul to Charon, she told him how sorry she was, realizing she, too, was in shock and unable to think clearly.

He seemed more confused than she. "Where are we going?"

"Tartarus. You know that. Are you okay?"

"Who am I?"

Her heart cramped in one painful knot. "What? Than? Thanatos?"

He blinked his ethereal eyes. "Therese? What a nightmare."

Tears of relief and regret rushed to her eyes, and in all two hundred thousand places she now journeyed with souls across the lands, she wept. She wept for Than, for what he'd endured. She wept for herself, wishing no one had to witness such an atrocious sight. And she wept with relief for the great fact that he was free for a whole year. The worse was over, for a while, anyway. As soon as she could graduate from high school, they'd be together. And although they'd have to go through this every year, she wouldn't think on that now.

"Therese?" Than whispered. "You okay?"

He'd just been ripped to pieces and he was worried about her? "Yes, Baby. Everything's going to be okay."

And everything would be okay, wouldn't it? As long as she could find her purpose.

When she and Than stepped onto Charon's raft, Ariadne and Asterion were stepping off to leave. They both gave her hateful looks. Her face went hot with embarrassment, but she didn't lower her gaze. Instead, she went closer to them and said, "I'm sorry. What I did to you was wrong. I promise to spend eternity trying to find a way to make it up to you."

Brother and sister looked at one another and then back at Therese with parted lips.

"I mean it," Therese assured them. "I can sense you're good, and I feel bad about wronging you. I will think of something, I promise."

Asterion and Ariadne looked back at her skeptically as Charon carried them off to the land of the living.

Than took her hand and said, "I love you." He bent his ethereal face down to hers and produced a barely perceptible kiss. She missed his body, his warm lips, but his soul would do for now.

Chapter Eight: Return Home

Therese disintegrated to lie beside Than's body while it awaited its soul, but it was so cold and so morbidly still that it gave her the creeps. So she kept Than's soul company in Tartarus while she disintegrated into hundreds of thousands to escort the dead. They mostly visited with Tizzie and Meg, and occasionally Alecto, who was usually hunting, until, on the third day, Than felt his body beckoning to him. Overjoyed, Therese guided him back to his chambers where he lay on his bed. His body was instantly warm and glowing once again: the union was complete.

Than sat up, but before he could stand, Therese pressed him back down with her enthusiastic embrace, lying partly on top of him as she covered his face with kisses. Now that the warmth and vitality had returned, she clung to his body, caressed it, moved her lips across his throat.

"I'm so glad you're okay," she murmured in between kisses.

"Sweet homecoming."

She felt the transference of duty from her to him, and her hundreds of thousands of selves reintegrated into the one. It was nice to be one again.

They played in bed for many hours, caressing, petting, kissing, until Therese felt the familiar pull of responsibility.

"I have to go back," she said.

"I know."

"Can't you come with me?"

"I'll come by later, okay? First talk to your family."

She'd been keeping a watchful eye over Clifford and Jewels, grateful to see her aunt and uncle taking such good care of them, but looked forward to being with them. After one last kiss, she god traveled to her bedroom in the middle of the night, gave her pets hours of love, surprised to discover she could understand them perfectly. They didn't communicate in words, but in ideas and emotions. Her Russian tortoise had missed her but had gotten to business by saying she had hoped for more lettuce and less carrots. She also hoped for more hibiscus petals and leaves, if possible. Clifford, her brown and white fox terrier, also had requests. His biggest demand was that she never, ever, leave him for so many days in a row again. He hadn't stopped trembling since she had left. And Carol and Richard were nice, but they didn't like going for long walks in the forest, nor did they remember to give him rawhide to chew on in the evenings. Plus, they wouldn't sleep with him, and he preferred a warm body to snuggle against.

Therese changed into a comfy pair of sweats and curled on the bed with Clifford, even though she didn't sleep. Having been a goddess for five whole days, she had learned that, although gods do sleep, it's not often. Than had said he slept once a month at most.

Clifford still wore a bandage on his head, which he scratched at when he wasn't licking Therese. When she asked if she could remove it, he panted with happiness. She tugged it off. He was healed, good as new, except for a little redness from where he'd been scratching.

No, she didn't sleep as she snuggled with Clifford, but she did do a lot of thinking. Foremost in her mind was what she would say to Carol and Richard. She hoped she could make it up to them in some way, but how?

Before she could come up with answers, she sensed Carol climbing the stairs and couldn't decide whether she should stay or disappear. The indecision was painful for fifteen seconds as she sat there, frozen, listening to Carol's footsteps. She had to face this sooner or later, so she may as well now. She quickly dimmed herself to mortal form and turned on a lamp, which she hadn't needed, able now to see in the dark.

"Therese?" Carol stood in the doorway, her hands at her mouth in shock. "When…how…"

"I didn't want to wake you." Therese moved to the edge of the bed and sat with her feet on the floor, not sure if she should hug Carol or stay put. "My bus arrived a while ago. I, uh, took a cab home."

Carol stood with her mouth agape.

"I'm sorry I left without telling you." Therese pulled at her hands, nearly ripping her own fingers off. She had to get used to her incredible strength. "I wanted to go someplace where people wouldn't look at me like I killed Vicki." Therese had been the one who paid for the ketamine, and everyone knew it. What had been meant as a near death experience in order to visit loved ones had turned into a disaster that was mostly her fault. "It's been hard enough without the cold stares, you know?"

Carol frowned. "You scared me to death. How could you hurt me like that?"

Therese dropped her head.

Carol rushed to her and put her arms around her, falling to her knees beside the bed. "You had me and Richard so worried. Than's dad didn't reassure me much."

Yeah, that conversation hadn't gone well, Therese recalled. What had Hades said? Kids will be kids? What can you do? Thanks, Hades. Thanks a lot.

Hades voice pierced her thoughts: "At least I spoke to her. Be thankful for that."

Oops. "Thank you, Hades."

"What?" Carol pulled back to look at her.

Had she said that out loud? "I mean, can you forgive me?"

Carol's face turned white and she rushed to Therese's bathroom and retched into the commode. Had she made her aunt sick with worry? Therese chewed on the inside of her bottom lip.

She followed her aunt to the bathroom. "Carol, I...I don't know what to say. It was stupid of me."

Carol wiped her face with a towel and turned to Therese. "What?"

"I didn't realize how worried you'd be. I didn't think."

Carol stood up. "Oh, sweetheart." She washed her hands and patted her face with cool water. "There's something I need to tell you. Let's sit down."

Therese returned to her bed. Carol sat on the edge of it, beside her.

"I was going to wait to tell you with Richard, but he's sleeping so soundly for the first time in days, so I won't wake him."

"Carol, what's going on?" Had they decided they couldn't handle her? After the drugs she'd done with Vicki and now running away, maybe they couldn't take having a teenager. She pulled Clifford into her lap. She'd be okay, right? She'd just go to Than, but the thought of them giving up on her broke her heart. Tears formed in her eyes, and she blinked them away.

"I'm pregnant."

Now it was Therese's turn to gape.

"I was going to tell you yesterday. Richard and I had planned something special for July fourth." Tears rushed from Carol's eyes.

That's right. It was Independence Day.

"We were going to take you to the park, to watch the fireworks. Then we were going to give you a gift from the baby." She wiped her face with the back of her hand. "These damn hormones."

"I'm having a baby cousin?"

Carol frowned. "Cousin and sibling. We adopted you, so, at least in the eyes of the law, this baby will be your brother or sister. Didn't you say you always wished you had one?"

Therese nodded, unable to stop the tears from streaming down her face. Yes. She'd always wanted a brother or sister. And now that she was getting one, she was leaving to join Than in the Underworld. She threw her arms around Carol, sadness gripping her heart. "I'm so happy."

The following day, Therese changed into jeans and boots and walked down to the Holts' place beneath a canopy of dark clouds to groom Stormy. She was surprised to find Courtney and Jen already there, doing her work.

"Hey," Therese said awkwardly.

The two girls turned in her direction.

"You're back!" Jen bounced from Sassy's side and threw her arms around Therese. "It's about time. Stormy's missed you."

With Courtney sitting on the stool in the stall, nuzzling the foal's nose, Therese felt doubtful, but she ignored her feelings of insecurity and gently reached out to stroke her horse—*her horse*. "Hey, boy. I've missed you, too."

Stormy met her eyes and neighed. Therese was shocked that she could understand him. "Where have you been?"

She ran her fingers through his mane. "I had to help out a friend. He knew your mother."

The petite brunette politely moved out of the way. "I'm Courtney, by the way."

Therese found it hard to meet her eyes, wondering if she blamed Therese for her cousin's death. When she did finally look, she found her dark eyes to be beautiful, reminding her of a famous French model she'd seen in her favorite magazines. "Hey."

Just then, Pete walked in, his blond hair framing his face down to his strong jaw. His blue eyes were full of relief. "I thought I saw you walking over. You're finally back."

Therese returned his smile. Dang, he was good looking for a mortal, and even by god standards. When he spread his arms for a hug, his flannel shirt slipped open, and sticking through his t-shit was what, an arrow? "What's that sticking out of your chest?" She crossed the barn but stopped short of the hug.

"Huh?" Pete looked over his t-shirt.

Therese realized it was Cupid's arrow. Mortal eyes must be blind to it. She stepped closer, pretending to brush away a piece of straw. "Been rolling around in the hay or something?"

Pete laughed and threw his arms around her. "I wish."

She felt the blood rush to her face and wondered, as he held her, if she could pull the arrow out. She wrapped her hand around it. Yes, it was partially tangible. She tightened her grip. Would it hurt him? What if it killed him? She decided to leave it for now, after she had a chance to ask Than. Maybe she could pull the arrow out of Pete's heart and spare him from suffering from a broken heart.

She stepped back from his embrace and patted his shoulder, nearly knocking him over.

"Whoa. Been working out?"

She blushed again. "A little." She had to learn to control her strength.

"Have you met Courtney?" Pete asked.

Therese nodded, but not without noticing Courtney's face light up when Pete said her name. Things just keep getting more and more awkward, she thought.

Later, after taking a shower and changing into clean jeans and a light sweater, Therese sat at the wooden table on the deck with Carol and Richard with a pair of binoculars in one hand. Dusk was settling, the perfect time to spot wild horses and other animals in the mountains across the reservoir. Plus, she was hoping she wouldn't have to talk too much about why she'd left. They already told her they expected her to swim in the championship meet tomorrow, even though she hadn't been to practice in over a week. The heat sheets were probably finalized anyway, so she wasn't sure she could swim in it even if she wanted to.

"Believe me," Carol had said. "The coach wants his top swimmer in this meet. He'll find a way."

Now, as Carol brought out a pan of brownies, she presented Therese with a gift bag.

"It's from the baby," Richard said. "I told Carol it was kind of corny, but you know your aunt."

Therese pulled away the tissue to find a multi-colored Coach handbag inside. "It's beautiful." Jen would kill for this, she thought. Therese liked it just fine but wasn't into designer accessories as much as her friend.

"Look inside," Carol said.

Therese opened the purse to find a matching wallet. "Thank you."

"Keep going," Richard said. "Open the wallet."

Surely the baby wasn't giving her money, she thought as she unsnapped the button and unfolded the fabric. Inside were dozens of clear plastic photo holders. Most were empty, but four of them held photos. The first was of her with her mom and dad, taken when she was six. She fingered their images, tears springing to her eyes. She'd forgotten how long her mom's hair once was, before she started keeping it short. And her dad's had never looked shorter. She gazed at his deep, brown eyes and warm smile, missing his arms around her.

Move on, Therese, she thought, biting her lip.

The second was a photo taken at her grandma and grandpa's in San Antonio. They were all in this one: her grandparents, mom and dad, Carol and Richard, Therese, and even Clifford and Blue. Her mom's mouth was open in this shot, like she was saying something to the photographer. Therese recalled that expression. She wished her mother was here, calling to her from the kitchen window with that same look on her face.

The third was from Carol and Richard's wedding last fall with Therese in between them. The fourth was a black and white blurry photo of…what?

"That's the baby," Carol explained. "That's a copy of the sonogram. That's how we were going to tell you."

More tears clouded Therese's view of the photos in the wallet, and she blinked them away, looking over the images again and again, not knowing what to say.

"We'll take more and add them in as time goes on," Richard said. "By the time you go to college, you'll have every one of those plastic slots full of your family."

Therese closed her eyes to fight the tears from turning into outright sobs. The idea of sharing her life with them and her new brother or sister sounded pleasant just then. She pictured the family vacations they might share, her little brother or sister always in her arms. Then later, when the baby was older, they could hike, canoe, bike, fish—all the things she'd always longed to share with a sibling. But it wasn't to be. Her place was with Than now. Neither the family photos nor the going off to college would become a reality.

"Thank you both. I guess I don't really deserve this."

"Enough talk like that," Carol said. "Let's put that behind us."

Therese nodded, desperately wanting to change the subject. "Speaking of school, I was thinking about going to summer school so I could try to graduate early."

"Why?" Richard asked before shoving a brownie into his mouth.

"Ever since what happened with Vicki, I've been dreading school. I just want to get it over with."

"If you really feel that way, why not attend school online?" Carol asked.

"What?"

"I don't know, Carol. Should we encourage her to run away from her fears?"

"No, but she's going to have to face her friends regardless of whether or not she attends high school. I finished my last two years of high school and my entire master's degree program online." Then she added with a wrinkled nose, "Don't like working in large groups."

Therese studied Richard's face for disapproval, but he appeared to be coming around to the idea.

"Really?" Therese asked. "You would let me do that?"

"Don't think it's easier," Carol warned. "The nice thing is it's competency based, so you work at your own pace. But the hard part is you have to be self-motivated."

Oh, she was definitely motivated. She jumped up from the table and hugged first Carol and then Richard. "This is the answer to my prayers."

"Hold on one minute," Richard said, taking her hand in his. "I want to make a deal with you first."

He sounded like Hades. She cocked her head to the side and waited.

"We'll let you enroll in an online school if, and only if, driver's education is part of your curriculum. We need you to learn to drive, Therese. We can't take you everywhere you need to go forever."

Drive? But she could god travel now. Too bad she couldn't explain that to them.

Therese glanced at Carol, who nodded. "Sounds fair to me. No more stalling, okay, sweetheart?"

Ever since her mother's car had plunged into Huck Finn Pond last summer with her and her parents inside...ever since she had to watch them drown before her, trapped in the car underwater...the idea of being in control of her own vehicle frightened her beyond reason. She reminded herself that she had sneaked past Ladon, outwitted the Minotaur, and faced the Hydra. She was a god now, for heaven's sake. But that didn't matter. She could still kill others. She hadn't been able to save her parents, and somewhere, deep down, she still felt responsible. She had killed her parents. She had killed Dumbo. She had killed Vicki. She could kill others from behind the wheel. Is that what she was afraid of? She didn't know, but she was definitely afraid.

Chapter Nine: Sweet Nothings

Than was waiting for Therese when she came upstairs after dinner. He wished he could have joined her and her aunt and uncle, but although he was no longer a threat to Therese, he continued to be to mortals. He envied Pete's ability to freely interact with Therese's friends and family. He'd watched them in the months since he left last summer. What made matters worse was the fact that everyone liked Pete, including Than.

"What's wrong?" he asked Therese as she plopped into the chair beneath her window without so much as a hug or kiss in his direction.

"Where do I start?" She folded her arms. "My aunt and uncle expect me to swim in the championship meet tomorrow, and I'm nowhere near ready. I haven't been to practice in ages. I'll probably let the whole team down."

Unbelievable. He lifted his palms up. "You're forgetting something."

"What?" She snapped.

"Wait for it."

A light in her eyes turned on. "Oh, yeah. I'm a god."

"Feel better?"

"Guess there's no doubt I'll beat Lacey Holzmann this time."

"Problem solved."

"But they're also making me learn to drive. I don't need to drive. But they don't know that. I can't very well tell them I can travel from here to China in a snap."

"What's the big deal?"

She frowned, obviously fighting off tears.

"Therese?" He scooped her into his arms and carried her to her bed. "Talk to me."

She stroked his hair, making him want to purr like a cat. "I don't know exactly."

"I have an idea." He touched the tip of his nose to hers. "And it's gonna be fun."

"What?"

"First kiss me."

Her lips tasted salty as he pressed his mouth to hers, her body warm against him. He missed the feel of mortal skin against mortal skin, but this was quite nice, too.

She ran her fingers through his hair, sending heat down his neck, his shoulders, his back. He rolled on top of her, keeping his weight off, then remembering she was no longer fragile. He sank against her.

"Oh my," she whispered, making him want her.

The phone rang. Therese looked at him. "I should get that. It's Pete. If I don't, Carol or Richard will just come up here."

He nodded and rolled off her. Of course it was Pete.

With his keen sense of hearing, he followed their conversation, which was yet another of the cowboy's attempt to get Therese out on a date. He didn't call it a date, of course. A group was going to the movies tomorrow night to celebrate the end of their swimming season.

"Yeah, sounds good," Therese said, to Than's surprise.

What?

She hung up the phone.

"You're going?"

"Why not?"

"Because Pete's in love with you."

"So? I can't help that. Talk to Cupid. Which reminds me. I can see the arrow sticking from his chest. Can I pull it out without hurting him?"

"That's weird. I don't see an arrow. You see an actual arrow?"

61

Her eyes narrowed. "You don't"

"No."

"What does that mean?"

"I'll find out. Meanwhile, why string him along by going with him to the movies?"

"Jealous?"

He wrapped a hand around her narrow waist and pulled her to him, side by side, face to face on the bed. "Damn right."

She bit his lip.

He bit back and then gave her a deeper kiss.

"Mmm," she moaned. "You have nothing to be jealous of. I just want to spend time with my friends before I leave them all, you know?"

He cupped her cheek. "Yeah. I get it."

"Besides, I haven't told you the worst news of all. The worst and the best."

"I'm listening."

"Carol's pregnant."

He sat up in the bed, confused. "How is that bad news? That's wonderful news." Then he added, "You don't feel like you're being replaced, do you? Because that's ridiculous."

"I hadn't thought of that, thank you." She got up and sat in the chair across the room.

Great. They were right back where they started: on opposite sides of the room. "Then what?"

"It's just, well…it's going to be even harder now to say goodbye."

He studied her sweet, worried face as a lump rose to his throat. So she was having second thoughts? After all they'd been through together? He didn't know what to say. Finally, he asked, "What are you thinking?"

"I'm thinking that on top of everything else, I have no idea what my purpose should be. Didn't you say it had to be unique? I can't be the goddess of animals, because that's Artemis. What about the goddess of friendship?"

"That's Philotes."

"Who?"

"She's one of the primeval gods, before Zeus and the other Olympians. Even before the Titans."

"There's nothing left for me, Than. How can I make this transformation stick if I never figure out my purpose?"

"You will." He tried to hide how unsure he felt.

They sat together in the silence for a while, Clifford moving from the bed to Therese's lap. She stroked Clifford, but Than could tell her mind was someplace else. He cleared his throat and said, "Let's get out of here."

"Where are we going?"

"You'll see."

Chapter Ten: Driving with Gods

Than took her hand and together they god traveled to an enormous building made of glass and filled with cars. Although the building was well-lit, both from the indoor lights and the outdoor floodlights in the predawn darkness, it was quiet and empty of people.

"Where are we?" Therese stood with Than on the ground floor gazing up at yet another level, visible from the open staircase, displaying the sexiest cars she'd ever seen.

"Sant A'gata Bolognese, Italy. The Lamborghini Museum." Than took her hand and led her around the cars. "Aphrodite drives a green one just like that one over there."

She followed his finger. "It's beautiful." She skipped ahead of him, pulling him along. "Look at this one. It's like the Batmobile. Rad, huh?"

"You prefer the Aventador to the Gallador?"

"I guess. Love the deep orange. How do you know so much about them?" They walked on, touring the gallery.

"I don't, but recently Aphrodite got me thinking. I took a brief ride in hers."

"Thinking about getting one of your own?"

"Our own."

Therese liked the sound of that. "As long as you're the one driving."

He squeezed her hand. "No, m'am. It's time for you to learn."

Just then, a flash of orange sprang from beneath the car nearest them.

"A cat," Therese said. "A tabby."

"It's frightened. Can you hear her?"

64

Therese nodded. She lunged to her knees and held her hands. "Hey, kitty. We won't hurt you."

Therese could sense the cat beneath the car, could hear her purring a frightened message: "I'm lost. I'm scared. I don't know where my boy is."

"We'll help you find your boy," Therese said. "Come out and talk to us."

The tabby poked her head from beneath a candy-apple red convertible. Tentatively, she padded a little closer to Therese, who sat back on her heels with her hands held out, Than standing close behind her.

"What's your boy's name?" Therese asked.

"Luis. He brought me here this afternoon and left without me."

"I bet he's looking for you." Than said. "The museum's closed tonight, but I bet he'll come back in the morning."

"I'm hungry, and thirsty, and scared."

Therese glanced up at Than. "Maybe we can find Luis."

Without warning, the tabby leapt into Therese's arms and then rubbed her face against Therese. She stroked the cat. "What's your name?"

"Belle."

Therese stood with Belle in her lap. "I have an idea." She turned to Than. "Listen to your human prayers. I bet a boy is praying that Belle isn't dead."

Than stared into space, apparently sifting through the multitude of prayers. At last he nodded. "You're right. I hear him. I know where he is."

Than took Therese's hand, and together with Belle, they traveled to a dilapidated townhouse in the historic district barely illuminated by one crooked streetlamp. Belle recognized the place and scampered from Therese's arms.

The two gods watched on as Belle pawed at the front door, and the surprised, gleeful boy who opened the door swept her up.

"Belle! You're back!"

A woman in a tattered nightgown stepped from the stoop and hollered, "I told you to get rid of that flea-infested parasite! What's she doing back?"

"I don't know," the boy replied. "Please let her stay. I'll keep her in a box outside."

"So long as she doesn't set foot in our house."

The tabby glanced back at the two gods just before Than took Therese's hand and led her back to the Lamborghini museum.

"Poor thing," Therese said, not feeling all that confident that the cat would be well cared for. "Maybe we should have kept her."

"The boy will make sure she's fed."

"Now that I'm a god, I can look in on her. I won't let her starve."

"Now, where were we?" Than asked.

She grinned. "So you're going to teach me how to drive, huh?"

"He's not." Hermes appeared like a flash between them. "I am."

Therese's eyes widened. "Hermes? Where did you come from?"

"Than disintegrated and persuaded me to meet you here."

Therese glanced at Than. Really? "You can't be serious."

"Why not?" Hermes quipped. "I am, after all, the god of travelers."

"I thought you were the messenger god."

"I am. And also of language, persuasion, animal husbandry, astronomy, commerce, and theft, among other things."

"Commerce *and* theft? Isn't that a conflict of interest or something?"

"Or something." Hermes put his fists on his hips.

Therese tipped her head back. "So you're to blame for the economy."

"Humans have free will, remember?" Hermes raised one wiry eyebrow. "Now do you want to learn to drive or not?"

"In one of these?" she asked. "Are we stealing one, then?"

"Just borrowing." Hermes winked. He turned and pointed to a long silver beauty. "That one. The Estoque. It's a four-seater."

Than opened the driver's door and motioned for Therese to climb in. "Ladies first."

"Um, that's okay. You go ahead."

"I insist."

Biting her lower lip, she climbed behind the wheel, reminding herself that they were gods, they couldn't be injured—at least not mortally—and they weren't on the road where others could be hurt. However, as soon as they were all comfortably seated and strapped inside, Hermes in the passenger's seat and Than behind him in the back, the landscape changed.

The sun was rising in a blue sky across rolling fields lined with rows of wheat. Cows grazed on other fields to their left from where they sat in the middle of a country road on the top of a hill.

"Don't just sit there," Hermes said impatiently. "Start the engine."

She felt for a key in the ignition, but there was none. "Uh…"

"Oh, for heaven's sake." Hermes rolled his eyes and the engine roared to life.

Therese clutched the steering wheel with both hands, her heart racing. With her right foot, she placed a slight pressure on the accelerator. The engine sped, but, otherwise, nothing happened. She looked at Hermes.

"Put her in drive first." More eye rolling.

"Sorry." She looked around the steering column and dashboard, only to have Hermes show her the gearshift on the console between them. She grabbed the end of it and tried to move it, but it wouldn't budge. She wrestled with it, breaking it off completely. "Oh, no!"

"You've been in this car less than two minutes and you've already broken it?" Hermes took the broken gear shift. "Where's Hephaestus when you need him?"

Warm blood rushed to Therese's face. "Look, I didn't ask you to do this."

Than's squeezed her shoulder. "I did."

"Yeah, but why?"

"Because I don't know how to drive either."

She studied his reflection in the rearview mirror. He seemed serious. Hadn't he done anything but escort the souls of the dead?

"Just so you know next time," Hermes said, holding the knob in front of her face, "you have to push this button in before shifting."

She turned to him sharply. "I'll remember that next time I'm driving a Lamborghini."

Hermes sighed. "That's true of most cars, Therese."

"Oh."

Hermes manipulated the shiny steel nub from which the stick had broken. "There. She's in drive. Now let's get started."

She eased on the accelerator again. When nothing happened, she pressed harder, gunning the engine.

"Parking brake?" Hermes asked with an impatient tone.

Therese lifted her foot as she looked around the dash. "Where is it?"

Hermes pointed to the knob. "Pull it. Keep your right foot on the brake. Then gently ease your foot onto the accelerator."

Therese did as he said and finally got the car in motion. She sped up to twenty miles an hour, feeling jittery.

"Take her up to fifty," Hermes said. "Looks like you've got the road all to yourself."

She eased on the pedal, unable to believe she was actually driving. "So where are we anyway?"

"Derbyshire, not too far from Ashbourne, one of my favorite towns. Hecate and I used to go fishing together there. So many good memories."

She glanced at the speedometer. "I'm at fifty. Now what?"

"Just get the hang of driving straight. Follow the road."

The road turned downward and then up as they passed sheep and more wheat. This wasn't so bad, she thought. Smiling for the first time since she'd climbed into the car, she let out the breath she hadn't realized she'd been holding. Her hands hurt from clamping the wheel, so she loosened her grip. Not too bad, she thought again, feeling like an adult. Up ahead, she noticed a sign indicating a deer crossing. "Why is the sign on the left side of the road?"

"Huh?" Hermes looked at the sign. "Oh, dear."

Before Therese could ask what was wrong, a big farm truck came into view heading straight for them. Why was it in her lane?

"What's going on? What should I do?" This was exactly what she was afraid of: killing someone. Her heart throbbed in her ears.

"Bloody hell!" Hermes shrieked, turning the wheel to the left.

The truck whizzed by them as Therese caught her breath and pressed on the brake, bringing the car to a choppy stop. All three plunged forward and then back in their seats.

"Forgot we're in England." Hermes gave her a sheepish grin. "They drive on the left side here. My mistake."

She looked at him with her mouth open. "That was close."

Another car came up behind them, sounding the horn and making her jump in her seat. Luckily it went around them, but not without giving them a furious glance.

"Get us off the road, Therese. Maybe we'll give Than a turn."

A little too slowly, she eased off into the tall grass on the side of the road. As she was about to climb out, Hermes grabbed her arm.

"You can god travel now, remember?"

"Oh, yeah."

She and Than switched in a flash, Therese falling back in the seat more abruptly than she had planned, having forgotten to keep her eyes open again. How long would it take for her to get used to her new abilities?

The landscape changed again, to a palm and papaya tree-lined street, narrower than the one in Derbyshire, and, here, the sun was at high noon. A volcano loomed on the horizon past fields of high grass where caribou were feeding.

"Take her over to the right lane," Hermes said. "We're on one of the Philippine Islands, where people drive on the right."

From the backseat, Therese watched Than maneuver the vehicle like a pro. "You sure this is your first time?"

"Positive."

"Why haven't you driven before? My god, you can disintegrate and do whatever you want. You never wanted to take a drive someplace?"

"Why, when I can god travel?"

She sat back in her seat. "I guess."

"And I have no problem driving my father's chariot."

"That's true."

"But you're right. There's a lot I haven't done."

"We can do it together."

"Have you chosen a purpose then?" Hermes asked.

"Not yet. Too bad you can't give me one of yours. You have a bajillion purposes."

Hermes chuckled. "Yeah. I used to have more before Thanatos and Hypnos were born. I used to do their jobs as well. Imagine that."

"I can't," Than said. "Don't know how you did it."

Than came upon a stop sign but pushed on the brake too hard and too fast, throwing Therese and Hermes forward and back.

"Sorry," Than said.

"Take a right here," Hermes said. "You know how to use the blinker?"

Than found it and made the turn. Then the car sped from thirty to seventy in a matter of seconds.

"Slow her down," Hermes said.

"I can't. Something's gone wrong."

Therese watched helplessly from the backseat as Than pumped the brake. The car turned a sharp left, just missing a group of people walking along the side of the road.

"Than, what's happening?" Therese cried.

Suddenly, gusty winds made the tall trees sway like hula dancers, and someone's hat flew past them.

"I don't know!" He continued to pump the brake and to wrench the steering wheel with both hands. "The Lamborghini's moving on its own. Let's god travel out of here."

"The car might hurt someone!"

"She's right," Hermes added. "We can't just abandon it. I sense another god at work."

They took another sharp turn to the left toward the sea. As they zoomed past little huts and a rickshaw toward a sandy beach, Therese was overwhelmed by a flashback of the evening her mom's car flew into Huck Finn Pond. She recalled the way her father, trapped by the steering shaft, had writhed and her mother, paralyzed by the bullet shot in her neck, had closed her eyes and yielded to the water overtaking them. She had been able to do nothing to save them.

The Lamborghini lifted up off the road, flew ten feet in the air over the sandy beach, and then plunged into the sea.

"Ahh!" Therese cried as the cold water rushed into the car.

"We're bound to the car!" Hermes said. "No god traveling out of this mess!"

Than reached back for Therese. "You okay?"

Before the car submerged, she felt herself being lifted at lightning speed up from the water, the Lamborghini falling away in a hazy mist. She rubbed her eyes and blinked, shivering in the cold wind. Sitting beside her was Poseidon.

Chapter Eleven: Poseidon's Warning

Than and Hermes sat in the seat just behind her as Poseidon held the reins of his chariot, drawn by Riptide, Seaquake, and Crest—three white stallions who flew across the water's surface at amazing speeds.

"Poseidon?" she asked. "What's happening?"

Hermes and Than leaned forward in their seats, Hermes shouting, "What in the world is going on, Uncle?"

"I'll explain when we get down to my palace." His long, sun-bleached hair, longer than hers, whipped in the wind, and his sunburnt face was set hard and unyielding.

They zipped high in the air above a volcano, Therese's stomach turning a flip-flop as she clutched on to the side of the chariot, her fingers cold, her knuckles white. Hair whipped in her face as she glanced back at Than, and her teeth chattered as she recalled the last time Poseidon had taken her for a ride. It had been as his prisoner to Mount Olympus. Maybe he never got over the fact that Artemis helped her win her meet earlier in the summer after Therese had turned down his offer. Maybe he'd been responsible for the earthquake that had damaged her school natatorium after all. The chariot flew in a chasm between two volcanoes and then out into the open sea. Therese glanced back again at Than to see his look of alarm, though his prayer to her was, "It's going to be okay."

In the next instant, the chariot submerged into the ocean depths. Therese was amazed to find she could breathe, and although she was cold, she wasn't freezing. Her body, like those of the other three gods, glowed in the darkness, creating a halo of light in which she could see the marvels of the sea around her. She could see beyond their glow as well, further into the darkness all the way down to the ocean floor. Though she passed by at nearly lightning speed, her goddess eyes could easily detect

73

everything—the colorful fish, coral, and shells, in addition to two curious nymphs astride dolphins who followed them, one on each side of the chariot. One of the dolphins was Arion, the dolphin on whose back she had ridden last summer. She waved, and he gave her a nod.

"Hello, again," he clicked.

She gasped, forgetting that she could now communicate with all beings, including dolphins.

"Hello!"

Up ahead, she could see Poseidon's palace. Worried as she was for his motives for bringing them here, she was nevertheless delighted to see it again. Bright golden lights came from the bottom of the ocean, illuminating the amazing transparent structure, its clear crystal walls making her think of an aquarium. Through the walls, she could see many figures inside of it—merfolk with tails and other, more human-like, people sitting among the furniture, eating at tables on golden chairs, and lounging on beds clustered in curtains of seaweed growing up from the ocean floor. At the back of the palace, the walls were no longer transparent and were made of shiny mother-of-pearl.

The three white steeds slowed and came to a stop inside a crystal chamber on the bottom level of the magnificent structure where three merfolk immediately swam over to unbridle the horses and lead them away. The dolphin-riding nymphs stopped outside the chamber and swam off, out of sight. Now that they were no longer in motion, Therese and the others floated up from their seats, and she had to continually pull her sweater down to keep herself covered. Despite this struggle with her top, Therese felt like she was in her element, having loved the water all her life. She'd started swimming at an early age, and her parents used to joke that she must have been a dolphin in a previous life. They didn't believe in reincarnation—at least not her mother. Therese had never been able to get a straight answer from her father.

Poseidon led them from what must have been the chariot garage, and they followed, swimming in their own fashion. Therese and Than swam breaststroke. Hermes, ahead of them, swam like a dog, paddling his arms and cycling his feet. Therese had the urge to laugh, and couldn't help it when she thought, "I don't want to make waves." The pun was corny, but she was nervous and excited and couldn't stop from giggling.

They entered a lounge with four couches facing one another in a square. Therese couldn't see how they would be able to sit on them, since all four gods floated on top near the crystal ceiling. But that problem was soon remedied when long tentacles reached out to them and handed them each a heavy boulder, save Poseidon, who was given his trident by a merman, and this kept him from floating. Therese followed the arms of the tentacles with her eyes to see the octopus on the floor between dancing rows of seaweed. She took the boulder he offered her and immediately sank to the floor with the others. She manipulated herself over to the couch next to Than and sat beside him. The couch was surprisingly comfortable and spongy, reminding her of a Temperpedic bed.

"You have our attention," Hermes said to Poseidon. His voice was clear underwater, as though he were speaking into Therese's ear through an earbud. "So tell us. What's the meaning of this?"

Poseidon sat on the couch directly across from Hermes. Than and Therese sat close together on a couch to themselves. "I've brought you here to warn you. I wanted to be safe within these palace walls with all my allies and servants at the ready. I couldn't speak of this anywhere else."

"Warn us?" Than asked. "Sounds serious."

Poseidon grimaced. "If you consider a plot by Ares to lock Therese into the depths of Tartarus with Cronus and his ilk serious, then yes."

Therese gasped, which made her gag on a bit of water. Than patted her back. She looked at him and asked, "Why? What could he gain by that? Does he hate me so much?" Tears sprang to her eyes.

"Not hate. Fear," Poseidon said. "He actually admires your loyalty and determination. He fears you as his enemy."

"But, but I still don't get why? How am I a threat to him?"

Than curled his arms around her more possessively. "It's not like we can vote on Mount Olympus. We're banished. We're out of the way. Tartarus? Really?"

"He doesn't want to see your union take place," Poseidon explained.

"That's ridiculous!" Therese said. "He just doesn't want me to be happy. Is that it? He wants to see me suffer!" The boulder rolled from her lap, and she started to float up again, but Than held her down. She took up her rock with both hands and returned it to her lap.

"He's not like that," Poseidon said. "He may love war and conflict, but he has no need for personal vengeance."

"Then why?" Than demanded.

"Gods beget gods," Poseidon said. "*You* may be banished from Mount Olympus, but your future children might one day skew the balance of power against him."

"Ah," Hermes said. "Now I understand."

Therese felt her face go white. She hadn't even thought of having children. That seemed so far away in the future.

"Can't we promise never to have children?" Therese wasn't sure she wanted to make such a promise, but it sure beat living eternity in fear of being captured. It sure beat remaining trapped at the bottom of Tartarus.

Hermes actually guffawed.

"What's so funny?" she asked with narrowed eyes.

Than turned to her with an awkward smile. "Um. Gods don't have birth control."

She almost said, "So?" but she caught herself. Oh. She could feel her cheeks turn bright pink. If they promised never to have children, they would essentially be swearing abstinence. No wonder Hermes laughed. What kind of marriage would that be?

"No more god travel," Poseidon warned. "It makes you vulnerable to abduction. Have you ever wondered why I prefer my chariot? Well, that's why. Most gods with something to lose prefer chariot travel. It's safer."

"What a pickle," Hermes muttered.

Therese swallowed more water, breaking into another fit of coughing as Than patted her back. When she'd gotten the water out of her windpipe, she asked, "Any idea how Ares plans to capture me?"

Poseidon frowned. "No. The only reason I know of his plan is that he asked me to do it. When I refused, he said no more."

Therese looked again at Than, wondering what they should do, but was only further worried by the expression on his face. His brows bent together, forming a v, his eyes were narrowed, and his mouth pressed into a tight line. She could see his jaw clenching against his cheeks near his temples. He looked like he was going to punch something.

"We'll get through this," she said to him, her turn to be the reassuring one. "It's going to be okay."

He stood up with his rock and paced. "Ares isn't getting away with this. I'll have my father block every entrance to Tartarus. My sisters will be on watch day and night. He can't control us like this. I won't let him. Damn him."

"We've got to find a weakness of his to exploit," Hermes said. "It's the only way. Even if he can't get her to Tartarus, there are other places to hold a victim."

"What weakness?" Therese asked.

"There's only one for Ares," Poseidon said.

They all looked at him.

"Aphrodite."

Chapter Twelve: Café Moulan

Than waited for Aphrodite in Paris on the patio at Café Moulan beneath the striped umbrella erected from the center of the round table. He was pissed that she could think of nowhere else to meet him when Ares could be right around the corner, where the two gods frequently rendezvoused. He supposed he'd rather Ares be in Paris than in Colorado hunting Therese. After Poseidon had delivered them in his chariot to Therese's house in the wee hours of the morning, Than hadn't wanted to say goodbye, but she had to compete in her championship swim meet today to maintain the illusion of being human. It was important that they keep Carol and Richard on their side. Therese would be unhappy otherwise.

Than clenched his jaw when Aphrodite finally pulled up in her lime-green Lamborghini half an hour late. He watched her graceful figure move through the tables on the patio, all eyes drawn to her, even though a scarf concealed her face. She exuded beauty in every feminine curve of her body, in the long golden tresses of hair gliding down her back. Than hid his frustration as she sat down across from him. As angry as he felt, he doubted he could carry out the backup plan Poseidon had suggested if Aphrodite could not help them: capture her in exchange for an oath from Ares to never interfere with Therese and Than's happiness again. Than didn't want to play that card if he could avoid it. Aphrodite had become his favorite aunt, and he didn't want to spend eternity on her bad side. He bit down his anger and frustration and said, "I ordered you a glass of wine."

"Wonderful." She took the glass and sipped. Then she sat back in her chair, crossed one leg over the other, swirling the wine in the glass between sips. "Why are we here?"

"I need your help."

She closed her eyes and sighed. "This has to do with Ares?"

Than nodded.

She gave him an exasperated look. "What's he done now?"

"He plans to capture Therese and lock her away."

"I thought as much. He doesn't like being out-numbered."

Than swallowed hard, embarrassed by what he was about to say. "If I promise not to touch her…"

Aphrodite's eyes widened.

Than felt the blood rush to his cheeks. "I love her. I'd do anything to keep her safe."

"Ares won't believe you. You're an oath breaker."

His lips twitched into a frown.

Aphrodite leaned forward, awkwardly averting her eyes. "Than, have you considered that maybe she'd be better off human?"

"Isn't it a bit late for that?" he growled.

"Not if she can't discover her purpose."

Than folded his arms across his chest, trying to suppress the mix of anger and frustration boiling inside of him. "So you want us to give up? After all we've gone through?"

"In time, she could be happy with the mortal struck by Cupid."

The anger blazed through him as he imagined Therese in Pete's arms. Then he recalled Therese's question about the arrow. "That reminds me. Therese can see the arrow in his chest and wants to know what would happen if she pulled it out."

Aphrodite pressed both hands against the table and leaned even closer. "She can see the arrow?"

Than lifted his chin. "So?"

"This is good news for you. Only a descendant of Cupid can see his arrows once they've pierced a heart."

"She was a demigod?"

"Not demigod. But she had some godly blood in her. Once the transformation took place, the sight of Eros came to her."

Than marveled at this revelation. He'd been impressed with her control over her dreams and her abilities with animals. "That explains a lot." He wondered again if they'd been fated to find one another. Had they always been meant to be together? Then he realized something else. "That means she comes from you and Ares."

Aphrodite flipped her long blonde hair from her shoulder and smiled. "I knew there was something special about her."

"Ares wouldn't hurt her knowing this, would he?"

She frowned. "She's too far down the blood line to matter to him. Many humans have some residual godly blood."

"But you just said she was special."

"Special because she comes from me." She leaned across the table. "Look, Ares was responsible for her parents' death. He can never trust Therese or her progeny not to retaliate against him."

"Then how is her relationship to Cupid a good thing for us?"

"There may yet be some undiscovered talents. And as to Peter Holt's arrow, she can't pull it out, but she might be able to shoot another in, to neutralize it."

"That would comfort her." And it was no lie it would put him more at ease as well.

"It could backfire and make him despise her."

Than sucked in his lips. He supposed hate was a better alternative to love.

"I'll speak with Cupid," Aphrodite promised.

"Meanwhile, you can do nothing about Ares?"

Aphrodite frowned. "There is one possibility."

"What is it?" A flicker of hope brought him to the edge of his seat.

"Ares once made a golden girdle for his daughter Hippolyta."

"The Amazon? I know. So?"

"Well, in addition to giving her the highest status among the Amazons, it also protected her from male attention. Whereas my magic girdle attracts men, hers protected her chastity."

"So you're saying he could make another girdle for Therese?"

"No. I don't think he would. It wasn't easy to make." She swallowed another sip of wine. "You could find Hippolyta's. It's been lost ever since Hercules took it from her as part of his labors."

"And once I find it?"

"Offer to have it permanently fitted to Therese."

Than sighed. To spend an eternity longing to make love to his wife would be a worse torment than the one imposed by the maenads, but if it was the only way to secure Therese's safety while allowing them to be together, well, he'd have to do it.

"Any idea where it might be?"

Aphrodite shrugged. "It was last seen during the war in Athens with the Amazons. Maybe Athena can help."

Chapter Thirteen: The Championship Meet

Therese stood in the locker room before warm-up showing Jen the new Coach purse and wallet Carol and Richard had given her. She flipped through the photos, lingering on the first one, the one of her and her parents.

"That was a sweet idea." Jen tugged off a pair of sweats and stuffed them in her locker with her flip-flops so that only her red Durango Demon swim team suit remained. "Just don't ditch me if it's a girl."

Therese tucked the wallet back into the purse and set it in her locker. "What are you talking about? I'd never ditch you." Guilt flooded through her, because that's exactly what she'd be doing once she graduated and married Than.

"You're *my* sister, too." Jen poked Therese's shoulder hard with her finger. "And don't you forget it." Jen walked away, ready to warm up.

Therese pulled her t-shirt off and over her head and folded it before laying it on top of her purse. Then she tugged her red swim cap over her head. Her face felt warm and her eyes moist. She was really going to miss Jen.

Lined up for relay, Therese glanced up to the stands once more and caught Carol and Richard's gaze. They waved again. She waved back. Pete, Bobby, and Mr. and Mrs. Holt were there, too, all looking down at the pool deck where she and Jen stood on opposite sides of the pool with the rest of their relay team.

The buzzer sounded throughout the indoor pool. Therese's teammate dove in for butterfly and maintained a hand's width distance behind the A-team swimmers for Pagosa Springs—Lacey's group. The backstroke swimmer widened the gap, leaving Therese's teammate in her wake. Therese was so distraught over this unexpected gap, that she forgot herself when she dove in for breast. She jumped off the platform with so much force and shot out across the pool with such speed, that by the time she landed in the water, she was only a few feet from the other side. Jen looked down at her from the deck in shock, gaping.

Someone yelled, "Go! Go, Jen! Go!"

Jen dove over Therese and took off, easily coming in first.

Throughout the rest of the meet, Therese struggled to keep a low profile, making sure to come in second and third for the rest of her races. Jen didn't mention the freakish dive throughout the meet, but everyone else couldn't stop talking about it. The coach said the word "Olympics" at least a dozen times.

Once they were alone in the locker room and changed out of their wet suits, Jen slipped on her sweats and flip-flops and turned to Therese.

"It has something to do with the crown, doesn't it?" Jen asked.

"What?"

"The dive."

Therese nodded, opening her locker for her t-shirt. That's when she discovered her purse was missing. Before she could respond, a voice called from across the locker room.

"Therese! What in the world?" The voice belonged to a teammate named Stephanie. "Look what I found in the trash can!"

Therese and Jen crossed the room and found Stephanie holding the photo of Therese and her parents.

Tears flooded Therese's eyes and anger clutched the back of her throat. "Who would do this?" She looked in the trash to see the other photos crumpled inside as well, even the sonogram. Had a god done this, or a human?

84

Later that afternoon while Carol and Richard were at a doctor's appointment for the baby, having another sonogram—this time to find out the gender—Therese was sitting on the couch in front of the television half-watching and half-thinking about the stolen purse when Than appeared beside her.

She threw her arms around his neck. "Hey, you," she said.

"I'm sorry about what happened today."

"At least I got the pictures back."

"Do Carol and Richard know?"

"No. It would break their hearts. I've got to try and keep it from them."

"Maybe I can find a replacement. Then they'll never know."

She popped up into an upright position, feeling perkier. She hadn't thought of that. "Aren't you clever?"

He took her back into his arms and kissed her. Then he said, "Listen. I've got some good news, some bad news, and some semi-good news."

"You met with Aphrodite?" She squared herself to him.

"She said only the descendants of Cupid can see his arrows."

"But we know that's not true because I can see it." Then she added, "I even felt it. It wasn't completely solid, but I could wrap my hand around it. Did you find out what would happen if I were to pull it free?"

"Therese. Stop talking and listen to me."

She rolled her eyes. "Than. I *am* listening to you."

"Only the descendants of Cupid can see his arrows."

"Like I said...wait." Did this mean what she thought it meant? "Are you saying...hang on, are you saying that *I* must be Cupid's descendant?"

"And Aphrodite and Ares's as well."

85

She jumped to her feet and waved her arms in the air, emitting a joyous whoop. This would let them off the hook, then, right? As much as she loathed Ares, he couldn't possibly want to capture her if he was her own ancestor.

"Wait." Than pulled her back down to the sofa beside him. "Aphrodite doubts this will change Ares's position, but what it does mean is that you can help Pete. You might even possess some talent we haven't discovered yet, something akin to your lucid dreaming and your ability to communicate with animals while you were still mortal."

She wasn't sure how to take this news. "Help Pete how?"

He explained what Aphrodite had told him.

"He could hate me?"

"Maybe. Maybe not. But it's better than letting him pine away for you, don't you think?"

"Better for whom?" she asked suspiciously.

"Him, of course."

He was right. Pete could move on with his life. She wouldn't be around anyway, so why did she feel sick at the thought of him hating her? "I suppose I'll need some practice first." She crossed her arms. "What's the rest of your news?"

She watched the blood drain from his face. Oh, no. More bad news? Her back stiffened. "Tell me." She braced herself.

"You remember how you said we could promise Ares we'd never have children?"

"Of course I remember. I got laughed at." Why did he have to bring it up? She felt her own blood drain from her cheeks in mortification.

"Well, there is a way."

Her heart sank. He was willing to give that up? "You mean abstinence."

He nodded. "Not my first choice, but, yeah." He told her about Hippolyta's golden girdle. "Aphrodite says we could have it put on you permanently, guaranteeing we could never…"

"I get it." She stood up and crossed the room. So she would live eternity like one of the virgin goddesses. "This is so unfair. You don't deserve this." She turned off the television, the annoying commercial making it even more difficult to hide her frustration.

"Neither do you. But I don't want to live in fear of your safety."

"It's so unfair."

"Life isn't fair."

Chapter Fourteen: The Parthenon

While Than gave Therese archery lessons in the afternoon in Colorado, he disintegrated and dispatched to Athens, where it was dusk, to meet Athena, who'd been summoned for him by Hermes, at the Parthenon. The ruins were no longer littered with tourists, so Than waited, alone, by the old statue of Athena.

Once Athena appeared, her raven hair barely visible beneath her silver helmet, her grey eyes brighter than the metal gleam above them, he told her about his plan to find the girdle.

"So Therese will join the ranks of the virgin goddesses," Athena said with an approving tone.

"If it's the only way we can be together without fear of Ares."

"Do you see those sacred caves across the acropolis from here?" She pointed to the west.

Than saw them. "I sense something dangerous dwells there."

"Yes. Do you remember Medusa?"

"Of course. Perseus cut off her head. It's there now, on your shield."

She lifted the shield proudly. "You know why I wanted it, don't you?"

"She and Poseidon met here at your temple."

"And soiled it with their love-making."

Than knew the story. Perseus himself had told it to him when he came to the Underworld. When Perseus cut off Medusa's head, their children, Pegasus and Chrysaor, sprang free. "Is it the giant dwelling in the caves?"

"Not Chrysaor, but another of her offspring formed from spilled drops of her blood. She's a serpent called Amphisbaena. She has a dragon head on each end. I brought her from the desert to dwell in the caves to protect my temple from further dereliction."

"What's this got to do with Hippolyta's girdle?"

"Amphisbaena is a seer of lost objects. The two heads don't always agree, but much insight can be gained from her. She might be able to tell you where the girdle can be found, especially if it exists somewhere in this region."

"Is she amiable?"

"No. But if you tell her I sent you, you might get her to cooperate."

"And if she doesn't?"

"You'll have to bind her two heads together and give her an elixir from Apollo. It will force the truth from her lips."

With his special power for summoning gods and delivering messages, Hermes located Apollo for Than more quickly than Than would have been able to find the god of truth on his own. Apollo lingered before a painting at an art gallery in Dallas standing beside his lover. In a black tuxedo, a fedora pulled over his eyes, a white scarf wrapped around his face, and dimmed to his lowest light possible, Than crossed the room, all the while sending his silent prayer to Apollo.

Apollo replied in like form that he was only too pleased to hand over the elixir, hoping for a speedy end to the conflict with Ares. As Than approached, he noticed how many of the patrons in the gallery allowed their eyes to linger on Apollo. Men and women alike couldn't stop looking at him and admiring his beauty. Even now, with his lover beside him, Apollo was greeted by two women competing against one another for his attention. Than wondered if he would have a similar effect on the living if he weren't Death.

"Absolutely," Apollo said to him silently. "You are quite stunning, you know."

"Thank you," Than replied, also in silence, as he grew closer to the god of light.

"But it can become dreary, attracting the attention of so many," Apollo said. "I try to avoid public places, but Marvin loves this artist. The painting is quite good, is it not?"

Than looked over the abstract movement of colors. He was surprised to find it reminding him of a melody, the way it lifted and seemed to sway one way and then another. "Yes, it is."

As Than reached him, Apollo took a vial tied to leather string from the inside pocket of his tuxedo and handed it to Than, turning his back on the ogling women. "Here you are, cousin." Then Apollo put a hand on his lover's shoulder. "You remember Marvin, don't you?"

"Sure. How are you?"

"Great. Thanks for asking. And you?"

"Not too bad, but I'm in a bit of a hurry." Than tipped his hat to the both of them. "Thanks again, cousin."

Now, armed with his sword and shield, a coil of rope around one arm, and the elixir on a leather string around his neck, Than returned to Athens to face Amphisbaena.

Chapter Fifteen: Piercing Pete

Therese reminded herself that no one else could see the arrow as she tucked it into the back pocket of her jeans and looked over her hair and makeup in her bathroom mirror. Jen and Pete were on their way to pick her up.

Carol and Richard still weren't back from their appointment and shopping in town. Therese had tried to call them on their cell phones, but had gotten no reply. Rather than freak out, she decided buying a crib and stuff for the nursery was probably taking longer than planned.

Than had shown her how to hold the bow and arrow, and though Therese had carried off a perfect shot on the first try, and many more since, she was nervous something would go wrong tonight when she tried to pierce Pete's heart with the special arrow from Cupid. After adding fresh water to Jewels's and Clifford's bowls, she folded the collapsible bow into her purse and headed downstairs.

"Wanna go outside, Clifford?"

He followed her to the back door and out onto the deck. She immediately sensed another presence.

"Who's there?"

She felt fear and panic gripping her chest, and this time she knew Ares's twin sons were close.

"Back inside, Clifford."

Clifford whined and followed her indoors, though a locked door would be no protection from the twins. "Than!" she cried.

Immediately he appeared in the kitchen beside her.

"Deimos and Phobos," she said. "They're right outside."

"I sense them, too."

The front doorbell rang. It was Jen.

"What do we do?" Therese asked.

"The twins won't touch you as long as you're in the company of mortals. They wouldn't risk Zeus's wrath."

"Therese?" Jen walked inside, looking around. "Hey, there you are."

Than had disappeared.

"Hey. I was just locking up." She checked the lock on the back door, grabbed her purse, and followed Jen out the front, hoping the twins wouldn't think of hurting her pets while she was gone. If they touched one hair on Clifford's body or one scale on Jewels's shell, she'd find a way to torment them.

As they walked to the truck, Jen said, "Matthew and I broke up."

Therese stopped and turned to her. "Oh, Jen. When?" Therese pretended like she didn't already know.

"Last week. The day you left. I didn't want to talk about it yesterday in the barn with Courtney there, though she knows. And I especially didn't want to say anything at the meet. Afraid I'd lose my focus."

"I'm sorry I haven't been there for you." She gave Jen a hug. "You doing okay?"

"I'll be alright." She pulled away. "We better get in the truck before Pete honks at us."

Todd, Ray, and Courtney met them outside the movie theater in the ticket line. Ray looked like he had a thing for Courtney. She hoped Courtney would give him a chance, though she seemed to prefer Pete. If she had the right arrow, could she play matchmaker like Cupid?

As they waited in line, they chatted and watched the people walking up and down the street, Therese still paranoid by the appearance of the twins. Deimos and Phobos wouldn't dare take her from a crowd of movie-going mortals would they? What about from a dark theater? She shuddered. Across from them was a café, and further over, a grocer, both well-lit and bustling with activity. The afternoon shower had left behind a residual coolness to the air, and Jen crowded close to her, warming herself with Therese's body heat. She heard Jen direct a prayer her way: "I'm so cold, Therese. Keep me warm."

Therese flinched, wondering if her friend knew she was communicating with her. Surely not, she thought, putting an arm around her, happy to have contact with a mortal. "Cold?"

Jen nodded.

A man walked by with his dog, a golden boxer with a brown head. Therese noticed them because the dog was muttering, "So unfair. So unfair."

Therese wondered what the dog meant. Testing her new abilities to communicate with animals, she sent a thought out toward the dog. "What's not fair?"

He looked at her with surprise, stopping in his tracks, and gave one short, desperate yelp. Therese understood it to mean, "My man beats me."

Therese gasped.

"What's wrong?" Jen asked.

"Look at that dog. He looks so sad."

Just then the man holding the leash jerked the dog, saying in a gruff voice, "Come on, you idiot. What are you stopping for?"

Jen and Therese exchanged looks of concern.

"He's a jerk," Jen said.

Therese watched the dog and his man continue down the street, wishing she could shoot an arrow into the man's heart and make him love his dog.

In the darkened theater in the middle of the center row, Therese sat between Jen and Pete, pretending to be interested in the bucket of popcorn in her lap, which the three of them were sharing. Courtney sat on the other side of Jen, with Ray and then Todd on the end. At first, Therese was disappointed she wasn't closer to Ray and Todd, since she hadn't seen them much this summer, but she realized not far into the movie that it didn't matter where she was sitting. All she could think about was piercing Pete. Her arrow of hate should neutralize Cupid's arrow of love so that when Pete looked at her, he would feel indifference. There was a chance the hate would be stronger than the love, since it would be the fresher wound. She fidgeted in her chair and mopped the sweat from her forehead with the back of her sleeve.

Her plan was to ask him to walk her to her door and then, when they were alone, she'd shoot him at such a high speed that mortal eyes couldn't detect it. Then she'd tell him she was getting back with Than and wait for his response. Hopefully he'd shrug and walk away.

When the time finally came and Pete was pulling into her gravelly drive, she said, "Pete, would you mind walking me to the door?"

"I'll walk you," Jen offered.

"Thanks, Jen, but I need to talk to Pete. Call me later. Maybe you can sleep over tomorrow."

Jen wrinkled her brow. "O-kay." Her tone carried a hint of sarcasm.

Pete turned off his truck and followed Therese to the base of the wooden steps leading up to her screened porch.

"Pete, I…" before she could say another word, he took her in his arms.

"Oh, Therese. I knew you'd come around." He showered her with kisses.

She pulled back, a bit too forcefully, forgetting her god-strength.

94

"Whoa," he said, stumbling back.

"I'm so sorry. I just want to talk." She whipped out the invisible, collapsible bow from her purse and cocked it in position. "There's something I need to tell you."

"What are you doing?"

Therese took the arrow from her back pocket and fitted it into the bow in less time that it took to take a breath. As she released the arrow into his chest, afraid of the finality of whatever consequences lay ahead, Jen ran up from behind him.

"Pete!"

"No!" Therese cried.

Pete turned toward Jen as soon as the invisible arrow struck, his eyes falling upon his sister.

"What do you want?" he growled at Jen. "You're interrupting!"

Jen stopped in her tracks and looked at Pete, bewildered. "What? Mom's been trying to get a hold of me. I've got a ton of missed calls from her."

"All our problems would be solved if you'd just go away."

Therese staggered forward. "Wait." Now what would she do? She couldn't have Pete hating his own sister. And she couldn't pierce him with a love arrow in Jen's presence and risk him desiring her. Her father was bad enough. Oh, god! She prayed to Than and to Cupid as the two siblings yelled at one another. What have I done?

"Take another arrow," Than prayed back. Then he appeared beside her, invisible to the others. "Tell Jen to wait for you in your room upstairs and pierce him again as he looks upon you." He disappeared, leaving her with the arrow in her trembling hand.

"Jen, Pete's upset."

"No shit, Sherlock," Jen snapped.

"Leave him alone for now. Wait for me in my room."

"He's never talked to me like that before. God, Pete. How can you say that to me?"

"Please," Therese begged. "Go to my room so we can talk. I'll be right there."

"Get out of here, Jen!" Pete hollered. "I can't stand the sight of you."

Jen wiped tears from her red cheeks as she ran up the porch steps. "Shut up already!"

Therese waited until Jen was out of sight. Then she fitted the new arrow to the bow and shot Pete once more. "Look at me, Pete!"

He wore a sneer, like a hungry wolf.

"Than and I are together again. It's for good this time. I just wanted you to know that."

Pete stomped toward his truck, snarling as he passed her, "Why don't you two bitches stay out of my life, okay? I'm sick of all the drama."

He drove off, leaving Therese stunned in the dark night. At least he no longer loved her. She heard a twig snap in the forest and rushed inside. The house was dark except for the small light over the kitchen sink. Carol and Richard must have already gone to bed. She went down the basement stairs to the garage to make sure Richard's car was back. Yep. Thank goodness they were alright. She headed up the stairs to her room, thinking it was good she wouldn't be alone tonight. She and Jen both needed one another's company but for different reasons.

Jen sat slumped on Therese's bed with a wad of tissues in her hand. Her eyes were swollen, her nose red. "Can you believe he said those things to me?"

Therese sat on the bed across from her. She couldn't let Jen think her brother hated her. Then she recalled what Hip had once told her: people have free will. The arrows only make stronger a feeling already present. Maybe Pete really did blame Jen for their family problems. If so, he was a jerk.

No. He couldn't have meant what he'd said. Therese knew Pete. "He didn't mean it. He was just mad and taking it out on you."

Jen wrapped her arms around herself, shivering like a wet cat. "He's never talked to me like that. He's been plenty mad before. What did you say to him?"

"That Than and I are back together for good. I thought he needed to hear it from me."

Jen sighed. "I need to call my mom. Can I sleep over?"

"Of course." It would mean Than would have to stay away, but she was probably safer with Jen, anyway. Deimos and Phobos wouldn't take her in the dead of night if she were lying by a mortal, would they? She doubted she would sleep.

"Broken heart or not, he shouldn't have said those things to me." Jen kicked off her boots and piled them in the corner of the room.

"I'm so sorry, Jen. There's something else you need to know."

Chapter Sixteen: Amphisbaena

The cool chill of night in Athens lingered in the air and wrapped its long fingers around Than, as though wanting to deter him from visiting Amphisbaena. The sacred caves in the underbelly of the acropolis smelled acrid and dank, and for once Than was glad his immortal senses weren't as sensitive to stimuli as mortal ones. With heavy boots, he trudged into the first of the caves searching for signs of the serpent dragon.

He could sense her presence, but couldn't pinpoint her exact location as he stole silently over the rocky cavern floor. A thin ribbon of water, stagnant and foul, divided the ground in half. Than straddled it as he followed it to the back of the cave. The first chamber opened onto a second, larger one, the size of an auditorium. He unsheathed his sword as he glanced around the cliff edges above him, feeling the serpent close. A billow of fire shot across the top of the cavern, and the residue of smoke lingering behind spelled, "I see you, Thanatos."

"Amphisbaena? I just want to talk," he said into the darkness.

Another flash of fire illuminated the cavern ceiling, and this time the smoke remaining spelled out, "Drop your sword."

Than gripped the hilt, fearing a trap. If he didn't drop it, he'd have to take her by force. "Can I trust you?"

The fire shot in a blaze above him, and the smoke read, "One says yes. Two says no."

"What is that supposed to mean?"

He waited for the fire, but when none came, he put down the sword. His fingers had barely left the hilt when the serpent darted from her lair and wrapped her thick, slimy body, at least a foot in diameter, around him, binding his arms to his sides. No matter how hard he pressed his arms against her, he couldn't get free of her ever-tightening grip. He disintegrated and grabbed his sword and was about to slice the serpent in two when a spider, the size of his skull, jumped on the end of the sword and spun a cocoon around him, trapping him. He disintegrated once more, in time to see the spider leap in all directions, from one side of the cavern wall to the next, weaving a web around the serpent. The moment he realized the spider was Athena, the web was cinched and the two heads of the serpent drawn tightly together. Fire spewed through the air from both dragon heads.

Athena transformed from the spider and commanded, "Release Thanatos."

Amphisbaena loosened her coiling body, and Than god traveled out while his third self cut his second self free of the cocoon. Then he integrated and faced Athena, sword in hand.

"I don't want her slain," Athena explained. "I've grown fond of her, and her screams would torment me."

"She's immortal, though, yes?"

"Yes. Unlike her mother," Athena replied. "Nevertheless, I intervened to protect her, not you. But I will help you get your answer."

"Why? Do you need something from me?"

"No. I only want peace among the gods. Hand me Apollo's elixir."

Than tugged at the leather strap around his neck and tossed the vial to Athena, who caught it and poured it into one of Amphisbaena's mouths.

"Ask your question," Athena said.

Than took a step toward the serpent. "Amphisbaena, do you know where Hippolyta's golden girdle is?"

Fire shot from both heads. The smoke on the right side read, "One says yes." The smoke from the left read, "Two says yes."

"Good. That's great," Than said. "Where? Where is it?"

The fire came again. The smoke on the right read, "One says Crimea." The smoke from the left read, "Two says Samsun."

Than narrowed his eyes. "But those cities are in two different regions. Crimea is part of the Ukraine. Samsun is on the northern tip of Turkey. Which is it, Amphisbaena?"

When the fire cleared, the smoke repeated the same message: "One says Crimea. Two says Samsun."

Than scratched his chin. "Is the girdle in someone's possession?"

The smoke that lingered read, "One says no. Two says no."

"Is it underground, lost among ruins?"

"One says water. Two says water."

"The golden girdle is underwater?"

"One says yes. Two says yes."

Than looked at Athena. "So the girdle is underwater near the shore of either Crimea or Samsun? That narrows it down, I suppose."

"Perhaps Poseidon can help."

"Yes. Good idea."

Chapter Seventeen: Mr. Holt

Before Therese could tell Jen what was on her mind, Carol burst through the door.

"It's a girl! You're going to have a sister!"

Therese jumped from her bed, a surge of joy sweeping over her. "A sister?"

Carol took her in her arms and gave her a squeeze. Then she pulled back, holding onto one of Therese's hands. "A sister. Are you happy?"

"Yes." She would have been happy either way. "A sister."

Richard could be heard ambling up the stairs, and in a moment, he popped inside. "Oh, hi, Jen. Are you sleeping over?"

"Is that alright?" Therese asked.

"As long as it's okay with her parents," Carol said.

"I was just about to call them," Jen said. "Congratulations."

"What do you think, munchkin?" Richard said to Therese, using one of many terms of endearment he'd called her over the past several months. "A sister sound good to you? You can teach her how to paint her nails and put on makeup and all that girl jazz."

Carol laughed. "Well, maybe not right away."

Therese laughed, too, adding, "I promise not to turn her into a diva."

"That's my area of expertise," Jen said.

"Some tomboy you turned out to be," Therese told her for the millionth time.

"Come down and see what we've been doing." Carol turned to the door, motioning for the girls to follow.

Richard, taking up the rear, said, "Don't you think we ought to warn her first?"

Carol stopped on the bottom stair and looked up. Therese stopped, too, wondering what the new look on her aunt's face could mean.

"Richard and I have moved into the master bedroom to make room in the guest room for a nursery. I'm sure your parents would have wanted that."

Therese's knees weakened, and heat rose to her skin. Of course her parents would want this. She knew it was the right thing to do. Nevertheless, her knees felt weak and she needed to sit down.

Jen caught her before she fell. "You okay?"

"Yeah. I'm fine," she lied.

They continued down the stairs to the guest room where Carol and Richard had been living all year. The walls had been painted a soft pale pink. Lacey cream window treatments matched the cushions on a corner rocking chair and the cream and pink striped bedding on the new crib. Over the crib, a brown teddy and block letters spelling "Lynn" adorned two low floating shelves.

"You're going to name her Lynn?" Therese asked.

"It's what I called your mother," Carol said. "I rarely called her Linda. So it seemed right to name the baby Lynn."

Tears filled Therese's eyes and she found herself unable to speak. She felt happy and sad at the same time.

Jen threw her arms around her. "That's so sweet."

Therese leaned on Jen, happy to have someone holding her up. Her knees still quavered. She cleared her throat, trying to rid herself of the lump lodged there. She tried again. "This room is beautiful."

Richard laughed. "So much for going gender neutral."

"That was the original plan," Carol explained. "But today, when we heard the news, well, I just went pink crazy."

"It's a pretty pink," Jen said, releasing Therese. "Not too bright."

"I like it, too," Therese added.

Just then the phone rang. Richard went to the kitchen and answered it.

"Oh, no. Of course. Absolutely. Sure. We'll be praying for him."

Therese followed Jen into the main room, with Carol close behind.

"It's my dad, isn't it?" Jen said without inflection.

Richard hung up the phone. "He's in the hospital. Your mother and brothers are with him. The doctors think he had a stroke and are running tests on him now."

"Oh my God!" Jen staggered to the sofa.

Therese sat beside her. "I'm so sorry."

Richard sat in the chair across from them. "Your mother wants you to stay here with us. She says there's no reason to go up to the hospital tonight. You wouldn't be able to see him anyway."

Jen put her face in her hands and wept, which surprised Therese. She thought Jen hated her father.

Carol sat on the couch on the other side of Jen and put an arm around her. "Is there anything I can get you? Do you want some water or anything?"

Jen shook her head. "I just want to go upstairs."

Clifford put his paws on Jen's knees. She scooped him up in her arms and kissed his head. "Thank you, boy."

She carried the dog upstairs. Therese followed, secretly thanking Clifford, too.

Once they were alone together in her room, Therese couldn't decide whether she should explain about Pete's arrow. Jen had accepted the invisibility crown without probing too hard into its origins; maybe she would accept the mystery of the arrow, too. But if Jen did press for more information, what would Therese tell her? Could she confide everything to her friend? Could she admit she was a god?

No. It would just freak her out, especially now, with her worried about her dad. Plus, knowing Therese would be leaving soon for good would only make Jen more upset. Therese also needed to consider the possibility that Jen would ask her to use her powers in ways that would make the gods of Olympus angry, like to heal her father. Just telling a mortal might bring repercussions. But she couldn't let Jen think Pete hated her. She had to think of something.

How could she be a god and still feel so helpless?

Chapter Eighteen: Dione

From inside the horse drawn carriage, Than gazed out at the raging Black Sea and the rocky shoreline rolling by as the driver above headed toward the northern city of Turkey known as Samsun. Because Amphisbaena's second head had been right about whether he should trust the serpent, he had decided he would try its prediction of the whereabouts of the golden girdle first. He crossed his arms, tired of waiting, wondering if Poseidon would stand him up, when, finally, the god of the sea appeared.

"Thank you for meeting me," Than said, before the other god had fully materialized.

"Don't thank me yet."

"Why not?" Than shifted in his seat and frowned.

"I cannot help you, Thanatos. I've already risked too much. Ares has been an ally of mine for many decades, and I can't afford to lose him."

"But I hope to appease Ares."

"Zeus also frowns upon any dealings with one of the banished. I won't get further involved. The sea is full of Oceanids, and if you call upon them, they may be able to give you the answers you seek."

Before Than could say another word, the god of the sea vanished.

He punched his fist against his seat. There was no way Than would allow Therese to be taken from him after they had sacrificed so much to be together. He would find a way without Poseidon's help.

When the carriage reached the outskirts of town, Than used the hilt of his sword to tap on the ceiling. The carriage stopped and Than climbed out, thanking and paying the driver.

"How will you get back, sir?" the driver asked.

"I'll walk."

Than turned grimly toward the sea, the rising whitecaps reflecting his angry mood. At least the wind off the shoreline offered him some relief from the humidity and heat. He hadn't dealt with many Oceanids in his life. In fact, he could count them all on one hand. He'd met Calypso when she tried to kill herself after losing Odysseus. Amphitrite, Poseidon's wife and the weaver of his golden nets, had come to Than once, demanding the return of a pod of dolphins which had died from being trapped in a fisherman's net. He couldn't help her, so he doubted she would want to help him. There were also his mother's three friends, the Sirens, whose deathly songs had brought him many souls, but he didn't trust anyone who lured innocent people into traps for their own entertainment. There were thousands of other Oceanids he did not know. Where to begin?

He hiked over boulders and sand to the end of a point where foam clung in white rings, took up a rock, and hurled it into the sea. The ocean was vast and deep. The girdle was the size of a woman's waist. He could disintegrate into a thousand parts and still spend years searching for it.

From the bottom of his heart, he asked the sea, "Is there anyone there who can help me?"

The pleasant face of a woman appeared in the foam near his boots. Silver hair and eyes shimmered against the rocks as she smiled up at him and said in a sing-song voice, "True love. So heartwarming."

"And heartbreaking," Than added. "With whom do I have the good fortune of speaking?"

"I am Dione. I'd know you anywhere, Thanatos. You, too, have broken many hearts by separating lovers with death."

"But I have no say in the matter."

"Who decides such things, then?"

"Usually, Tyche, the goddess of chance, an Oceanid and sister of yours, I believe. I've never had the pleasure of meeting her."

106

"You give her too much credit I think."

"Perhaps." He didn't want to displease a nymph who'd possibly come to help him. "How is it you know so much about broken hearts?"

"My daughter is the goddess of love."

Of course. He'd heard of Dione. Few gods on Mount Olympus acknowledged her role in Aphrodite's existence, wanting to subjugate the daughters of the Titans. Both Aphrodite, daughter of Dione, and Athena, daughter of Metis, had had their histories rewritten with sole credit of their parentage attributed to Zeus. Only Hades, least happy with his lot and most concerned with justice, had mentioned their names on rare occasions.

"I recognize your name now," Than said, bending to one knee. "My father has spoken of you. He prefers you to some of your sisters."

Dione smiled at that. "You speak of the Sirens."

"Yes."

"And yet they add souls to his kingdom."

"In ways unjust and that cannot be avenged."

"Ah."

"My father often says that life isn't fair, but death is."

"How noble."

Than didn't know if justice was nobler than compassion, but he kept the thought to himself. Plus, he may have detected a touch of sarcasm in the nymph's tone. "I'm looking for Hippolyta's lost golden girdle. The serpent seer, Amphisbaena, believed it to be underwater either off of this coast or that of Crimea. Do you have any knowledge of its whereabouts?"

"No."

Than sighed and closed his eyes.

"But I can ask around. Maybe someone else has seen it."

Than smiled at the nymph in the foam and thanked her.

"But why do you care for an old girdle?" she asked.

He explained his problem with Ares.

"I'm saddened to hear that. One of the surest ways to weaken true love is to have your true love wear it."

Than climbed to his feet. "I hope she'll never have to cast eyes on it, but I'm desperate to have her in my life any way I can."

"I see. If I learn anything about the girdle's whereabouts, I'll send my courtier to find you."

He followed her eyes to the sky and saw a white gull, her courtier, flying overhead. Before Than could reply, Dione disappeared from the foam.

Chapter Nineteen: Baby Lynn

Therese spent the next several days with Jen visiting Mr. Holt in the hospital and grooming Stormy and Sassy. She avoided Pete, who continued to snap at Jen about the most trivial things—like who woke up earlier or ate the most food. His attitude toward Therese seemed to settle on indifference. This was what Therese had wanted, but it still hurt. Carol helped Therese enroll in an online high school, and she had already completed her first assignments. She was amazed by how quickly she absorbed information. By no means omnipotent, she nevertheless understood and memorized concepts and facts so quickly that she was flying through her courses. Than stayed with her at night, keeping her updated on his progress in his search for what she had come to call the item of doom. Since she didn't need as much sleep as she had as a mortal, she had a lot of extra time to worry about her future, like what her unique purpose would be. Would she ever figure it out?

And she constantly looked over her shoulder for the twin sons of Ares.

After a week's time, Mr. Holt was placed into an assisted living center in Durango because his stroke had left him paralyzed on one side of his body, and he needed more care than Mrs. Holt and her kids could give him. Therese thought Jen would be relieved, even thrilled, with this, but, instead, she was depressed, saying that her mother and Bobby would now be miserable. Somehow Jen blamed herself for her father's condition, which made no sense to Therese. Maybe Therese didn't have all the information she needed to understand Jen's feelings, but whenever she asked Jen about it, her friend clamped up.

On top of feeling guilty for her father's condition, Jen was depressed about her breakup with Matthew. Worst of all was her treatment from Pete, the big brother who had always stood up for her in the house when no one else would. So even though Therese was burdened by her own fears and concerns, she had to be strong for Jen.

She distracted Jen over the next several weeks by inviting her to do things with her. Part of Therese's new curriculum required her to accumulate service hours, so she convinced Jen to go with her to the animal shelter they used to volunteer at back when they were in the Girl Scouts in the fourth and fifth grades. Even though Therese hadn't gone to the animal shelter regularly since then, she had continued to volunteer there a few times a year, and the employees remembered her. They also volunteered at Mr. Holt's assisted living center on Sundays, running games like Bingo and Jeopardy. After their third visit, Therese had an idea.

The idea came from a paper she was writing for one of her classes on the use of animals in therapy. The therapy ranged from children with autism to the elderly. Therese shared her idea with Jen, and together, they convinced both the assisted living center and the animal shelter to allow them to take two well-behaved dogs, Bo and Meatball, to visit the elderly at the center every Sunday. They developed a routine in which they worked at the animal shelter on Saturday and took animals to the assisted living center on Sundays. Jen led Bingo or Jeopardy while Therese supervised the pet therapy, and then during the week Therese worked on her studies and groomed Stormy. At night, she and Than spent time together. Some evenings, she and Jen went to the movies with Ray, Todd, and Courtney.

Pete no longer joined them and their friends on their outings.

Besides looking for the item of doom, Than was also helping her to figure out how to reverse the effects of the arrow on Pete's attitude toward Jen. Cupid had no answers and Aphrodite was looking into it.

110

She also discovered, weeks after Than had found her a replacement Coach bag and wallet, who had stolen her purse. It had been a mortal after all. In late August, when marching band camp began, Jen recognized the purse on Gina Rizzo's shoulder. She called Therese that night.

"Maybe Gina bought one like it, but it looks just like the one you had. I thought you should know."

She thanked her and hung up, but was surprised to find she wasn't angry. If Gina really wanted that bag, let her have it. She was hurt that her precious photos had been so carelessly thrown away, but thankfully, she had them back. She saw no reason to confront Gina. Jen tried to change her mind, offering to help, but Therese wasn't interested. She laughed a little at herself over this. Here she was a powerful goddess finally able to kick some ass, and she no longer wanted to.

Her mood was further lifted by the fact that she had saved a two-year-old yellow lab from being euthanized by convincing Todd that his yellow truck would look even better with a yellow dog. Ray and Todd had come to the shelter to take a look at Chuck while she and Jen were there volunteering.

"Chuck is short for Chuckles," Therese had said. "We call him that because he's always happy."

Then just about the time when Therese thought things might be getting better, they got worse. She was home cooking dinner for Carol and Richard. She wore her favorite t-shirt and faded pair of jeans with holes in the knees, which reminded her of her father. Than, supposedly guarding her from the evil twins, was a distraction with his flirtatious kisses and booty slapping as she bent over the oven to check on her spinach lasagna. When they heard Richard's vehicle pulling up on the gravelly drive, Than gave her one last kiss goodbye with promises of seeing her later that night. Therese hummed cheerily as she mixed the salad and got out the dinner plates. But when Carol and Richard walked in, she could tell by their tear-stained cheeks and red-rimmed eyes that something was wrong.

"What's happened?" Therese asked, nearly dropping the plate in her hand. What could possibly be wrong now?

"Come and sit down." Richard helped Carol to the couch. "We need to talk."

Had they learned Therese's secret? Were they mortified to discover she would soon be joining the god of death in the Underworld? What else could have them so fragile-looking and defeated?

Therese emptied her hands and moved to the living area to sit across from them, pulling her knees up to her chest and hugging them.

"We have some bad news," Richard said.

Carol hadn't even looked at her yet. Oh, God. This was not good.

"There's something wrong with the baby," Richard said in a broken voice.

Therese dropped her feet to the floor and sat up. "What? What's wrong? Is everything going to be okay?"

Carol shook her head. Without looking up, she choked out, "No. I'm afraid not."

Therese felt her chest tighten and her hands and feet go numb. Was there a ringing in her ears? "Why? I don't understand."

"It has to do with Carol's placenta. Apparently, the baby isn't getting enough nutrients and isn't growing properly. The doctor said odds are Lynn...won't make it."

Therese sat quietly, dazed and unable to believe. She felt like she was looking down at herself from the ceiling and recognizing how helpless she looked. But she was a god now. There was bound to be something she could do, some other god she could bribe. Athena had saved Sahin. Someone must be able to save Lynn. Hera was the goddess of marriage, family, and unborn children. She would go to Hera.

She jumped to her feet. "I won't let this happen."

Carol crumpled into a ball of shaking sobs in Richard's arms at Therese's defiant tone.

Therese stroked her arm. "I'll think of something. There must be something we can do."

"Calm down, pumpkin," Richard said. "Just take a breath and calm down. This won't help your aunt. You've got to be strong. All we can do is wait and see."

Therese dropped to her knees at Carol's feet and took one of her hands. "I'm going to think of some way to save Lynn, Carol. I promise you."

Carol gave her a half-smile, with quavering, wet lips. "Oh, sweetheart. There's nothing you can do but pray." She kissed Therese's hand before breaking down into more tears.

Therese hugged them both, stood up, and said, "I know you probably don't feel like eating, but maybe you should try, for Lynn. Everything's on the table. I've already eaten." That last part was a lie, but she wouldn't be able to eat now. She had to figure out a way to help her sister. "I'm going upstairs."

Than was waiting for her in her room with open arms. "I'm so sorry."

She sank against him and wept harder than she had since the day Than was ripped by the maenads. He held her close, caressing her hair. He kissed her forehead, her cheek, and the top of her head. Then she stood up, wiped her eyes, and said, "I'm going to see Hera. I don't care how mad she is at us, I'm going."

"You can't go to Mount Olympus."

"Oh yes I can." She clenched her fists and lifted her chin, feeling the power rising inside her.

Than's eyes widened at her resolve. "Well, at least let me take you in my father's chariot so you don't risk god travel."

"I'll wait for you outside."

"Are you sure about this?"

"Absolutely. Please hurry."

"I'll be right back."

Chapter Twenty: Hades

Than entered his father's chamber, having decided to ask for, rather than take, the chariot. He and Therese were already going to be in so much trouble when they showed their faces on Mount Olympus. He didn't need to add to their problems by stealing a chariot, too.

He knew his father was in his worst mood at this time of year after having been bereft of Persephone's company for five long months. On September 21st, she would finally return, but until then, Hades would be irritable.

His father sat at his table across from Meg in a whispered conversation when Than arrived. The two of them stopped talking and glared up at him.

"Sorry to interrupt."

"Then don't," Hades said.

"Therese and I are going to Mount Olympus tonight."

Hades narrowed his eyes. "Good luck with that."

"I need to borrow your chariot."

"Take it. It's yours."

Than looked from his father to Meg, her blonde hair usually up in a knot now spilling down her shoulders. He asked, "Is everything alright, Father?"

"Nothing's been alright since you first laid eyes on that girl."

"What's going on? It concerns me, doesn't it?"

Meg averted her eyes, but Hades climbed to his feet. "It seems Ares never intended to take Therese to Tartarus. That was a decoy. We've been monitoring the pit every minute of every day, wasting valuable resources when he's been hatching another plan."

"What plan?" He looked at his sister. "Tell me." He wondered if Poseidon had been duped by Ares or had been working with him to throw them off the real plan.

Meg stood now, too. "We don't yet know."

"But trust no one."

"Do you think it's unwise, going to Mount Olympus?"

"It's the safest place for you. Ares would never take her in front of the other gods."

"Even though we disobey Zeus in going?"

Hades tugged at his beard. Then he put a hand on Than's shoulder. "I'm no seer, son. I don't know how Zeus will react." He lowered his voice, "So you're finally standing up for yourself? I'm glad."

Than glanced again at his sister, but her expression told him nothing. "It's Therese. She wants to ask Hera for help."

"She's got some nerve," Meg said.

"I like it," Hades added. "Take the chariot and go."

Than bridled Swift and Sure to the golden chariot, wondering over his father's reaction. He really wanted Than to stand up to Zeus? In what way exactly?

Chapter Twenty-One: Storming Mount Olympus

Although the chariot was invisible to mortal eyes, they had to fly it high in the Colorado skies to avoid the tree-covered mountains. The air was crisp and the stars bright and the moon only a sliver, like the shiny hilt of a sword. Therese wished she hadn't lost hers at Lerma with the Hydra— not that she would have used it to attack. She clutched the locket from Athena at her throat. She was a god, and she could do this.

"What's the plan?" Than asked.

"I don't know yet. I'll make it up as I go." What more could the gods do to her? Turn her over to the maenads? She'd do anything to save her sister.

She was glad Than hadn't tried to talk her out of this, hadn't forced her to articulate her motives and expectations. She was thankful he sat beside her with the reins, supporting her in silence as they sailed across the night sky. If only she could think of her purpose before facing them, then she'd feel less temporary, less transient. What could she do? Hermes had so many purposes and Artemis had all Therese's favorites. She loved music, but Apollo had that covered. Even her ability to maneuver through the water was out-mastered by Poseidon. What talent did she possess that could possibly add anything new to the roster of gods and goddesses?

"Help me think of my purpose," she said. "There's got to be something I can do."

"Only you can discover it."

"You've got to have some ideas. Anything?"

"Your gift with animals is remarkable."

"But Artemis has animals."

Than leaned over and kissed her nose. "You don't have to figure this out right now. Quit being so hard on yourself."

Than was such a good person. The gods were wrong to keep him from Mount Olympus. He may have broken an oath, but they were wrong to make him take it. They hadn't *asked* him to swear on the River Styx never to make her a god; they had *told* him he must. There was a difference. And their demand was simply not fair.

She decided not to tell Than about her second reason for facing the other gods. She wanted to save her sister, but she wanted to save Than, too.

If it could only be as easy as saving Chuck, the yellow lab. Wait a minute, she thought. She looked at Than, her mouth and eyes wide open. Saving animals. Not wild animals, because that was Artemis. Saving animal companions.

"What?"

"I know what my purpose is!" She waved her fists through the air, full of excitement. "I know what I'm meant to do!" She jumped to her feet.

Than pulled her back down in her seat. "You're going to fall out of this thing. Now sit down and tell me."

She spread her arms wide. "Meet the goddess of animal companions."

"The what?"

"You know how Cupid shoots arrows into people to make them fall in love?"

"Yeah?"

"Well, I'll shoot arrows into humans and their animal friends to make them love one another. I'll help save rescue animals by piercing the hearts of visitors when they come into the shelters. Don't you see?"

"You'll rescue pets. That's you to a tee."

118

"And I'll stop animal abuse by piercing the hearts of the abusive owner!"

"Like that man you told me about and his pit bull."

"Boxer."

"That's right."

"And I'll help reunite lost pets with their humans."

"Like we did with the tabby."

"Oh, Than! I know this is what I'm meant to do! I just know it! Artemis shouldn't object. She's the goddess of wild animals. That's totally different!"

Than dropped the reins, took her face in both hands, and pressed his mouth hard against hers. The chariot took a sudden dive toward the land, so he snatched the reins back up, laughing. "You're so great, Therese. I knew you'd figure it out. I can feel your power emanating from you. The transformation is complete!"

"Zeus has got to listen to me now. He's got to!"

When they reached the summit of Mount Olympus, Than guided the chariot to the outer gates and said, "Spring, Summer, Winter, and Fall, open the gates of Olympus so Therese and I, Thanatos, may enter."

A face appeared in a gray cloud, female and beautiful with black-lined eyes and an equally black-lined mouth. She blinked long lashes and smiled upon them. "I'm afraid we cannot open the gates for you, Thanatos."

Therese stood up in the chariot. "Listen. We need to speak with Zeus and Hera. I want to explain why they were wrong to banish us, but I can't do that if you don't let us inside."

"Sure you can," the cloud replied. "Through prayer."

"You want to explain what?" Than interrupted. "I thought we were here to save your sister."

119

Therese turned inward, to her mind, and directed a prayer to Zeus. "I need to talk to you in person. We've traveled a long way. Please let me make my case to you and to your queen, Hera. Plus, I need to claim my purpose!"

The cloud moved from the gate, saying, "You may enter, Therese, but Thanatos must remain outside the gates."

"I go everywhere she goes," Than insisted, standing.

The cloud returned to the center of the gates. "Goodbye then."

"Wait!" Therese squeezed Than's hand and looked up at him. "I know you want to protect me, but I'm a god now, too. Let me go alone."

"You don't know what Zeus is capable of, what he's done to other gods in the past."

"I need to do this. Trust me. Please."

He took both her hands in his. "You're sure?"

"Never surer."

She kissed him hard on the mouth and then stepped from the chariot and walked through the gates and across the courtyard to the steps of the palace. When she entered the court, all gods were present, including Hades and Poseidon, who were usually in their respective palaces. She hadn't expected a full audience. Even Ares was there. She glared at him wishing she could hurl something at his smug face. Now was not the time to pick a fight. She'd take on Ares another day.

Her throat felt dry as she walked to the center of the ring of gods and faced the double throne where Zeus and Hera sat, but she swallowed hard and said, "I've come here for three reasons. Please hear me out."

"Speak," Zeus said, his manner and look reminding her of Hermes. His curly hair and beard were darker than those of his brother Hades but exactly the same as the god of both commerce *and* theft.

"First, I've found my purpose. I'm the goddess of animal companions." She turned to face Artemis. "Not of wild animals. Not of the hunt. I'm talking about tamed animals meant to live with humans. As a descendent of Cupid, I've shown I can use a bow and arrow. My job will be to pierce the hearts of humans to make them love their pets, and vice versa, and also to help them when they've lost one another."

"Bravo," Artemis said. "Well done!"

"Congratulations!" said Athena.

"Wonderful news!"

"Congratulations!"

Therese turned slowly around the circle to meet the eyes and congratulations from each of the gods. She filled with pride, the corners of her mouth spread wide. All but Ares seemed happy.

"Thank you." Therese felt confident and more powerful than ever. "Now for my second purpose for coming here tonight. The only reason Than swore an oath on the River Styx was because you made him do it. He had no choice."

"He most certainly did," Zeus objected.

"Not a real choice. When you hold a gun at someone's head and tell them to do something or you'll shoot, is that someone truly free? No. When you tell a woman give me all your money or I will kill your child, does she freely give it? No. You coerced him by giving him horrible consequences if he refused: My death. That's no choice, Zeus, and you know it."

"Now just one minute, Therese, goddess of animal companions," demanded Zeus.

"Please let me speak. I have more to say." Therese widened her stance, setting her feet firmly on the marble floor. "Than is a good person. He has served all of you and humanity for centuries without a single complaint. He has the most loathsome job of all of you." She looked upon each of the gods surrounding her. "Would any of you say otherwise?"

No one replied.

"I thought so. I've been taking classes lately, and I've had the opportunity to study what humankind knows of you. I've learned that all of you have done things you aren't proud of, except maybe Hestia, who lives her life serving the rest of you."

Hera gasped.

"I won't allow such insolence!" Zeus shouted. A crack of thunder sounded above them. "You may be one of us, but no one comes to court pointing an accusing finger at me."

Therese felt her knees weaken, and she thought, *Oh, crap! What have I done? Now they're all against me!* But she clenched her fists and kept her stance.

Before she could speak, Hades was at her side. "I say we hear her out. Isn't her fierce ability to stand up for someone she cares about something we gods value?"

"Hear, hear!" Persephone cried, and a smile was exchanged between husband and wife.

Zeus looked down his nose at Therese and pressed his lips tightly together. He stared at her with an expression that said he was not pleased. She held her breath, wondering if she had just made the biggest mistake ever. Maybe she should have come on her knees begging for mercy.

No. She knew she was right.

She didn't wait for an invitation to continue. "Like I said, nearly all of you have done something you're not proud of. I'm not here to accuse, but merely to point out that this is the first time Than has done anything that might be considered wrong.

"And think about it. He did it because he wanted what everyone wants: Someone to hold his hand. Someone to love him forever, no matter what. We all want that."

"What are you asking us to do?" Zeus demanded.

She took a breath and said, "He broke no real oath. He deserves no punishment. No maenads. No banishment. What he went through with the maenads already is more punishment than he deserves. I want you and the court to reconsider your decision."

"Impossible!" Ares objected.

The gods broke out into quarrelling among themselves, some nodding, others shaking their heads, and all Therese could think was, *Crap, crap crap! This isn't going the way I envisioned!*

"Quiet!" Zeus commanded. The voices stopped and all looked at the king of the gods. "I'll discuss this matter with the others once you leave, but I make no promises of another outcome."

"Thank you." Therese turned to Hera. "I came for one final reason. I want to offer my services to Hera in return for a favor. My aunt is pregnant and the baby, my sister, is in jeopardy. Hera, can you save her? I'll do anything you ask of me."

All eyes were now on Hera. She glanced around the room, apparently delighted by the attention. "There is something I want. If you can get me this thing, I will save the baby."

Therese's heart burst with joy. "Name it."

"I want my golden apple back from Artemis!"

Therese couldn't help but think how petty this queen of the gods could be. She would demand an apple when she had hundreds? Therese hid her distaste.

Now all eyes turned to the goddess of the hunt.

Artemis pushed a stray brown hair back from her face and crossed her arms. "Well, I...I'm not giving it back."

Again, Therese was filled with disgust over the pettiness of these gods. She resolved to never become like them, heartless and selfish. Her baby sister's life was in danger and these two were quibbling over an apple?

As if Artemis read her mind, the goddess said, "Thousands of humans die each day, Therese. You must understand that the birth or death of one more baby doesn't move me enough to give up an apple that has the power to transform whoever eats it."

"Name your price," Therese said, her heart pounding against her ribs. "One thing I've learned from Thanatos is that everyone longs for something. What do you long for, Artemis? I'll do anything."

"What I want, you can't give."

"Try me. Tell me what it is."

The goddess of wild animals walked across the marble floor to the center of the court and faced Therese. "Not here." Then Artemis prayed, so the other gods couldn't hear her, "Maybe you can help me. And if so, I will give up the apple. But what I want must remain a secret between you and me. I'll come to you soon in the forest by your home."

Chapter Twenty-Two: Artemis's Tale

When Therese turned to leave the palace on Mount Olympus, she felt something press against her back. She reached over her shoulder and found a quiver full of arrows.

"I don't understand." She glanced at the gods around the room. "Is this a gift?"

"No." Hades took her elbow and ushered her to the door. "The quiver and arrows magically appeared when you declared yourself."

"They aren't from Cupid?" They descended the rainbow steps.

"No. They came from *you*." He led her past the whale fountain and out the gates to Than.

Than helped her into the chariot. "What a relief. What happened in there?"

"You should be proud of her, Thanatos."

"I am, but perhaps you should tell me why."

"As the poet John Donne once wrote, rarely can a man find a woman both true and fair. Therese is as loyal as she is beautiful." He kissed her hand. "I'll be glad to one day call her daughter." Hades disappeared.

Therese turned, open-mouthed, to Than. "Can you believe that? He kissed me."

"I knew it wouldn't take long for everyone to see you as I do."

She circled her arms around his neck. "Take me home."

He kissed her cheek and stroked her hair. "Let's go, but tell me what happened on the way."

Over the next several days, Therese spent much of her time walking through the woods behind her house, begging Artemis to show herself. Without mortal company, she was no longer safe from Deimos and Phobos, but she had to risk facing them if she was to meet Artemis and save her sister. She carried the collapsible bow given to her by Cupid, and slung across one shoulder was the quiver of arrows, feeling as natural there to Therese as if they had grown from her body. They must be meant to serve in her new purpose as goddess of animal companions, but she didn't know if they could protect her from enemies. If the twins appeared, she'd find out.

She conveyed these thoughts to Artemis in the form of prayer, pleading with her to appear and share her secret. Therese didn't know how long the baby had to live, so every minute was precious. "Please, Artemis. I'm here." She stole up the path, paying special attention to the surrounding cypresses, since those were the hunter goddess's favorite trees. But each day and night, Artemis did not come.

During this time, Therese was also inundated with prayers from people around the world who had lost their pets or who were worried about their pets' health or behavior. She prayed to Zeus to grant her the power of disintegration so she could more efficiently respond to these prayers, and he prayed back that he would consider her request. Meanwhile, she'd sworn to Than, Poseidon, and Hermes that she wouldn't god travel, so the only thing she could think to do was to inspire them by planting ideas in their psyches. "Look in your neighbor's shed," she whispered to one regarding a lost puppy, and, "Don't feed him gluten," she whispered to another whose cat had allergies. She was pleased when people took her inspiration to heart and solved their problems but was frustrated when others didn't seem to hear her.

She also sped through her online courses, passing exams with perfect scores. At this rate, she would have her degree in less than a year.

During the day, because Carol was on bed rest, Therese did most of the cooking and cleaning around the house. Although Richard helped out, his job as a freelance reporter sometimes required him to leave to conduct research, including interviews. The solemn mood in the house was oppressive, so Therese didn't mind stealing away to pick through the forest with Clifford. Most of the time, they went at night, before or after a visit from Than, while Carol and Richard slept.

One night, well past midnight, in her sneakers, black jeans, black t-shirt, and black winter cap pulled low over her head, she crept past the twin elms and climbed up the path through the pines and cypresses with Clifford, when a sinking feeling came over her as it occurred to her that Artemis's instructions to meet her in the forest might be a trap. Could it be a coincidence that the goddess of wild things chose the very woods in which Ares's twin sons had been stalking her for weeks? She pressed her back against the trunk of a tree and took a deep breath. Clifford sat on his haunches near her feet. *Focus*, she told herself. *Use your new senses*. She closed her eyes and reached out with her consciousness, feeling for the pressure created by the presence of other beings. She felt the chipmunks in the trees, the deer yards away in the shrubs, the birds in nests overhead, and the insects in the wood and earth. Further up the mountains, she sensed a family of bears, but, like every night since she left Mount Olympus, she sensed no other god.

Then the ground beneath her opened up and she fell into the crack. Although she landed firmly on her feet, she winced in surprise. Her head was level with Clifford, who barked ferociously beside her. She followed Clifford's gaze to see the twins standing over her with their fists on their hips and smiles on their faces.

"What a foolish girl you are," Deimos said.

"She decided to make this easy for us," added Phobos.

127

Fear and panic threatened her, but not as overwhelmingly as when she was mortal. She took an arrow and fitted it to her bow.

The twins looked at one another and guffawed.

"Should we feel threatened?" Phobos mocked.

Deimos laughed so hard that Therese could see tears forming in his eyes. "Maybe we should run for our lives, brother."

"That's right. She looks so frightening."

They held their bellies and continued to laugh at her.

She took aim and shot Deimos in the heart. Without pause, she fitted another arrow and shot his brother. Upon penetration, both gods turned into miniature dachshunds. She fitted another arrow, just in case they transformed back into their original forms. Clifford growled, baring his teeth, and the two dachshunds whined. Clifford sprang for them, but the twin dogs vanished.

"Bravo," came Artemis's voice from a nearby tree. "Nicely done."

Therese aimed her arrow at the shimmering cypress. "So you didn't come to trap me?"

"I came to tell you the most important story of my life." The tree fluttered, and in the next instant Artemis stood above her, her leather boots level with Therese's eyes. "The saddest story of my life." She waved her hand over the ground and a stump emerged. "Have a seat."

Therese returned the unused arrow, noticing others remained in the quiver, as though she hadn't already spent two. Realizing they must regenerate, like skin cells, she leaped from the crack in the earth to stand on solid ground beside her dog. "We made a good team, Clifford. You deserve praise as well." She scratched his back. Then she sat on the stump and patted her thighs. Clifford jumped onto her lap. She was grateful for his warm body and friendly face as she wrapped her arms around him, her heart returning to its normal steady rhythm after its panicky flutter during her encounter with the twins, and listened to the goddess's tale.

"Centuries ago, I met my one, true love. Her name was Callisto, one of many nymphs who kept company with me, hunting in the woods, running foot races, picnicking beneath trees. We began as friends, but, over time, we grew to love one another, and we swore we would remain pure and true to each other forever."

Therese knew precisely what it felt like to swear your heart to another and wondered what could have happened to have made the two lovers part. She kissed the top of Clifford's head.

"But one day while we were bathing together in a warm spring with a handful of other nymphs, I noticed she was with child. Can you imagine my horror, my heartbreak, my rage?"

Therese would have crawled inside a hole to die, but goddesses don't die. "What did you do?"

"I made her leave my company and all our friends. I told her to go away and to never return." She tucked a strand of her brown hair back up into its knot and wiped a tear from her cheek.

"So you never saw her again?"

"No." Artemis's voice cracked. "Soon after, I learned Zeus had tricked Callisto into having relations with him."

"Tricked her? How?"

A single tear slipped down Artemis's cheek from a forest-green eye. "He disguised himself as…me."

Therese widened her eyes in surprise. Zeus had raped Callisto. Once again, her shock and disappointment over the behavior of the gods gave her the resolve to be better than they. "Callisto was innocent. She never broke her vow to you."

"No."

"So what did you do?"

"I went everywhere looking for her, but after weeks of searching high and low, I learned Hera, full of jealousy, had turned Callisto into a bear."

"A bear? But it wasn't Callisto's fault. Hera should have turned Zeus into a bear!"

"Sshh. Lower your voice. We can't be overheard."

"Sorry." She nestled her chin against Clifford's head. "Go on."

"I continued to look for Callisto, but I was no longer sure what she looked like. I couldn't sense her. And I was scared a hunter would kill her."

"Is that what happened to her?"

Artemis folded her arms and shook her head. "The son she bore almost killed her by mistake when he was sixteen and out hunting, but Zeus intervened and turned him into a bear as well. Then he flung them both high into the heavens where they became Big Bear and Little Bear, or Ursa Major and Ursa Minor."

"The constellations?"

"That's right. They possess asterisms more commonly known as the Big Dipper and the Little Dipper."

"And Callisto's there still?" She wasn't sure how that could be, since the stars were light years away.

"Yes. For all these centuries. A day hasn't gone by that I haven't longed for her company, or a night that I haven't stood gazing up at her, begging her to forgive me. If I'd given her a chance to explain, I might have protected her from Hera."

Therese didn't know what to say. Artemis was right.

"That's why I took Hera's apple. I tried to use it as a bargaining tool to force Hera to give me back Callisto, but she claims she can't. I've also heard the apple can return a person back to his or her original state, but I have not been able to figure out how to get her from the sky without upsetting the universe."

It would be impossible, Therese thought. "That *is* a sad story, Artemis. I'm really sorry for you. But I don't understand what you would have me do."

"The Big Bear is one of the circumpolar constellations in the northern hemisphere, meaning it rotates around the North Star. For centuries, it was the only of these constellations to never reach the horizon."

"I still don't see…"

"Just listen. You've heard the tilting of the earth on its axis has changed over time, haven't you?"

"Yes?"

"So in more recent years, Callisto's feet have touched the Aegean Sea, especially in autumn."

"And this is important because…"

"In order to have the apple, you must reunite me with my Big Bear now that she can reach the earth."

"How do you propose I do such a thing? You yourself haven't been able to, and you're more powerful than I am."

"Perhaps as the goddess of animal companions, you will find a way. That is for you to determine. But tell no one. I can't risk Hera getting wind of it." Artemis vanished.

Chapter Twenty-Three: Goddess of Animal Companions

For the rest of the night, Therese researched the Ursa Major constellation on the internet and considered how she could possibly take Big Bear out of the sky. She sat on her bed with her laptop across her legs and Clifford curled up beside her, asleep. The prayers of pet owners everywhere distracted her from her research, and she took time to inspire as many of them as she could, but knowing Baby Lynn could die any day forced her to make Artemis's quest a priority.

Than seemed hurt when she asked him not to come tonight, but he said he understood. As promised to Artemis, she did not tell him the details, only that she didn't know if she could succeed, but that she had to try.

She learned the Big Dipper was used for centuries to find the North Star and to help nighttime travelers find their way. If she pulled it from the sky, how would they find their way and what would people think? Maybe they would assume the end of the world was on its way, as they had when the Mayan calendar ran out on December 21, 2012. Worse than their confusion would be the impact on the universe and the gravitational pull between the planets, stars, and other space matter. Big Bear couldn't just disappear from the northern skies without repercussions.

Damn Hera for requiring her apple, and damn Artemis for not freely giving it. She swore to herself once more that she would never allow herself to become the kind of goddess who put her needs before everyone else's.

But wasn't that what she was doing? Pet owners everywhere were praying to her for help, and her top priority was saving her sister. Was she no better than the other gods? A bead of sweat formed on her forehead. She closed her laptop and sighed.

Why shouldn't she help herself first? Was it a god's responsibility to serve others foremost? She had the power to help, but did she also have the obligation to make helping others her number one priority?

Before she could answer her questions, she heard a scream. She brushed her laptop to the bed and jumped to her feet. Faster than the time it took a human to blink, she grabbed her bow and quiver and was at the foot of the stairs searching for Carol. The scream came again, and this time, she realized it wasn't Carol, but Jen, and the scream wasn't coming from inside Therese's house, but through Jen's agonizing prayer.

"Should I call you, Therese? What am I going to do?" Jen's fervent prayer was followed by another wail.

The early dawn light streamed in through the kitchen window. Carol and Richard were likely asleep. Therese scribbled a note for them, leaving it on the kitchen bar, and then ran at her full speed to the Holts' place. She arrived within seconds.

Not sure whether she should knock at the door, storm inside, or fly up to Jen's window, Therese paused on the front porch. The scream came again, but louder, blood-curdling. She stormed through the door.

The chaotic scene unfolded. In less than a second, she took it all in: kitchen chairs overturned, dishes smashed all over the tiled floor, a red stain splattered on the wallpaper in the breakfast nook, the light fixture over the table still swinging as though something had hit it minutes earlier, and sprawled on the kitchen floor, blood spilling from his arm, was Pete. He looked at her without speaking, apparently in shock, flat on his back, breathing like a runner. On the other side of the room, Jen stood with a pistol in her trembling hands, lowered and pointing to her feet. Tears streamed down her face.

"I had no choice," Jen said through labored breaths. She was a blubbering mess. "He was going to kill me."

"Where's your mom? And Bobby?" Therese crossed the room and took the gun from her friend's quavering hands.

"On the way to see Dad. After they left, Pete attacked me."

Therese helped her to a chair. "I'll take care of him." She put the gun in her back pocket and rushed to Pete's side. He was losing blood fast. "You're going to be okay."

He turned his crystal blue eyes toward her but did not speak.

"I'm so sorry this happened." She kissed his forehead. "It's all my fault." She prayed to Apollo as she took a dish cloth and wrapped it around Pete's arm. Apollo replied that he was tied up and could not come. She prayed to Than, but he reminded her that his presence would only ensure Pete's death. Then she had an idea.

She stood up and fitted an arrow to her bow. As the arrow shot, Jen jumped from her chair and screamed, "What are you doing for God's sake?"

The arrow struck Pete in the chest, alongside the other two, and he transformed into a beautiful golden retriever. Jen looked at Therese with wide eyes, started to say something, and then fainted across her chair.

"Good," Therese muttered. She didn't need Jen in her way. She knelt beside the injured dog and unwrapped the towel from the wound. She focused her energy on healing him. Maybe her powers as goddess of animal companions would extend to healing.

"What's happening?" Pete asked though his new dog mouth.

At first nothing happened, but then she noticed the bleeding stopped. She applied more pressure to the wound with her towel. When she lifted the towel, the wound remained, but it looked less serious. She stroked the dog's belly and said, "You're going to be okay." She stood over him with another arrow.

Jen opened her eyes and stumbled toward her. "What are you doing? Where's Pete?"

"I need you to trust me. Can you do that? I gave you the crown, didn't I? Can you trust me?"

Jen stared back dumbly and nodded.

"Come stand in front of me. I need Pete to see you first."

"What? Where is he?"

"I'm right here!" he growled, but Jen couldn't understand him.

"Come over here Jen, so the dog can see you."

The dog whimpered as Jen approached.

"It's okay, boy," Therese said, taking aim. "Stay still, Jen. My timing has to be just right." Therese released the arrow, and in the split second before it struck, she ran out the front door so the only person Pete could lay eyes on was his sister.

Therese paused outside the house for a moment before returning to Jen's side. The dog had climbed to his feet and was now licking Jen's hand.

"Where did he come from?" Jen asked, unable to see the arrows sticking out from the dog's chest. "And what happened to Pete? Did an ambulance come?"

Therese's shoulders relaxed with relief. "Yes. Pete's at the hospital. I called 9-1-1 while you were passed out. The paramedic told me to tell you to get plenty of rest."

"Am I in trouble?"

"No. I told him it was an accident. Now go upstairs and get some rest. I'll find out if this dog strayed from the Melner Cabin or something."

"What about my morning chores? The horses?"

"I'll help you with them later. Go back to bed."

Jen padded across the room to the stairs, still somewhat shaky, and climbed up to her room while Therese kept Pete from following her.

"It's okay, Pete," Therese whispered. "You'll see her in a minute. And I'll get you back to normal as soon as I can."

"I'm so confused. I'm not sure who I am anymore."

"You're going to be okay." She knew her arrow hadn't infected him with desire, because her arrows were meant to bond human and animal companions with platonic affection. But she couldn't leave him as a dog, and if she could transform him back into a person—and she hoped beyond hope she could—she worried over what his feelings would be for Jen. She also wondered if he'd recall what Therese had done to him.

She stroked his fur for many more minutes, giving Jen time to get in bed and fall asleep. Then, after a half hour had passed, during which she continued to inspire pet owners who prayed to her, she fitted another arrow into her bow, wished he'd become human, and shot him.

Nothing happened. The golden retriever looked back at her, as though he hadn't felt the arrow penetrate. Then he turned from her and trotted up the stairs, limping on his left front leg, which though better, wasn't healed. Therese followed. The dog went directly to Jen's bedroom and curled beside her sleeping form. Jen started awake and saw first the dog beside her and then Therese bending over them.

"What's going on?" Jen asked.

"Can he stay with you awhile, just until I find his owner? He seems to like you an awful lot."

"Sure." She smiled sleepily and pet Pete.

"I'll call your mom and tell her about the accident and let her know everything's okay. I'll tell her Pete cut himself real bad."

"But she'll find out you lied."

"Not if Pete goes along with it, which he'll do after the way he's been treating you." Therese met the golden retriever's eyes, daring him to say differently. "I'll clean up, too. You just go back to sleep now. I'll see you later."

Therese returned downstairs to call Mrs. Holt and clean up the mess. She also tucked the pistol away in a kitchen drawer. Then, at a speed approaching that of light, she cleaned the barn and groomed the horses, including Stormy, speaking to them in soft tones so as not to spook them with her inhuman movement.

She could sense Carol and Richard were awake, so she flew to her bedroom window. Than was waiting for her.

"I couldn't change him back!" she cried as he swept her into his arms. "I really thought I'd be able to do it. How stupid could I be?"

He pushed a strand of her hair behind her ear. "At least he no longer wants to kill her."

She pulled back, gripping his shoulders with both hands. "But he's a dog!"

"Calm down. I know a way."

"You do?" She wrapped her arms around his neck and kissed him. "Thank god! Tell me."

"Hera's apple. It's been used before to transform a beast that was originally human."

That's right. Artemis had said as much. "Should I try to take another from the garden of the Hesperides?"

Than crossed his arms and sucked in his lips, thinking. He shook his head. "Hera won't save Lynn if you do."

Then she realized something else. She dropped her arms to her side and lowered her eyes, feeling hopeless. More tears fell on her cheeks. "Hera won't give me an apple. And if I succeed in Artemis's quest and then get the apple from her, I can't transform Pete *and* save Lynn. I'll have to choose."

"Maybe Pete and Jen are better off…"

She snapped her head up, eyes wide. "I can't leave him in the body of a dog! It's my fault. I changed him! I've got to change him back. It was the only way I could think of healing him and reversing his hate for Jen. I knew I could help animal companions and make them love their humans. That's why I did it. But I truly expected to be able to change him back. Ugh!" She opened one of her bedroom windows and leapt out.

Chapter Twenty-Four: Vanished

Than followed her out the window. "Wait up!"

He used his keen vision to scan the perimeter but could not find her. "She better not have god traveled." He reached out with his consciousness but could not sense her. He prayed to her, "Where are you?"

She replied, "I don't know!"

His body stiffened where he stood on the ground outside her house. "What happened?"

She did not reply.

"Therese?"

Nothing.

He god traveled directly to the gates of Mount Olympus demanding to be let inside.

The gray cloud refused him.

He pounded against the golden gates and screamed in frustration. "Zeus! Let me in! Ares has taken Therese! Let me in, our you can find someone else to guide the dead!"

The gray cloud floated up in fear, but the gates did not move. Than disintegrated into the hundreds of thousands and, as one huge mass, charged the gates. They barely budged, but the tiny gap he created was large enough for one to slip though. The hundreds of thousands of Thans pressed against the gates while the one entered. He reintegrated and charged across the courtyard and up the rainbow steps.

Hephaestus worked in his forge and Hestia in her kitchen. Hades and Persephone were absent—autumn having arrived because his mother had returned to the Underworld. Artemis was also gone, and Demeter had returned to her winter cabin. But the others were seated on their thrones visiting among one another, Poseidon with Apollo and Hermes, Hera with Zeus and Ares, and Aphrodite with Cupid, who had come in from tending the stables. They all looked up when Than entered like a bull from its gate. He ran at Ares and wrapped his hands around his throat.

Ares laughed.

Than disintegrated into five and surrounded the god of war, each taking a limb and disabling him. "Tell me where she is, you coward."

"Or what?" he asked. "You'll rip me apart as the maenads did you?"

"Good idea."

Zeus stood before them in his full form and bellowed, "Release my son!"

"Not until he tells me where he's taken Therese!"

"How dare you speak to me in this manner, Thanatos!" Zeus roared.

Zeus's army of three Cyclopes, larger and stockier than any among them, entered the palace, ambling across the marble floor in their slow, ungraceful gait. One by one, Arges, Brontes, and Steropes peeled each Than from Ares and threw him to the ground. Than responded by continually disintegrating, despite the painful blows. Like a colony of ants from its hill, he kept multiplying until the Cyclopes wailed in anger and frustration. Than had never turned against the gods before, and now he realized his special power of disintegration gave him a unique advantage. He would never attempt to use it to overthrow the Olympians, but he would fight for Therese.

"Enough!" Zeus shouted.

The other gods looked on, some with concern and others with amusement.

The Cyclopes stopped and ambled from the palace.

Than integrated into five and maintained his hold on Ares, who was no longer laughing.

"Get this repulsive god away from me!" Ares wailed.

Than took great satisfaction in having bested the god of war, if for even a little while. "Tell me what you've done with Therese!"

"She's not been harmed, only taken," Ares growled.

"Return her you mother f…" Than looked up at Hera and thought better of his words. "You weasel!"

Ares strained against him but could not break free. "On one condition."

"Name it."

"You find Hippolyta's girdle and let me fit it to Therese."

Than wanted to strangle the god, and he tightened his grip around Ares's neck. "What have I ever done to you?"

"Besides threaten to break my neck?" Ares mocked.

"Tell me where to find the girdle."

"I've been looking for it, but with no luck."

"Let her go. I promise to search for it. I promise not to touch her. Please." Than released Ares and integrated. He stood before him.

Ares rubbed his neck and gave Than a hateful glare. "You find the girdle and I'll set her free."

Than glanced at each of the gods present in a circle around him. "Will no one help me?"

All but Zeus lowered their eyes, even Hermes, whom he loved like a big brother.

"You're an oath breaker, Thanatos," Zeus said. "You've lost our respect."

Than looked at Aphrodite, whose face was pink and whose mouth was turned into a frown, but she did not look back. Cupid, too, avoided his eyes. These were Therese's ancestors. Didn't they care for her safety?

141

And Ares, also from the same blood, was to blame for all of this! He glared up at Zeus. None of this was fair.

Just as he was about to give up on all of them, Athena stepped forward. "I will help you, Thanatos."

"As will I." Hephaestus came up from behind and put a hand on Than's shoulder.

Chapter Twenty-Five: The Amazonian Pit

Therese's arms were bound behind her back. She was blindfolded and sat on a surface that felt like dirt and rock. Something blocked her from being able to stretch out her consciousness to see beyond the blindfold, to god travel, and to pray. She could hear Than's frantic prayers to her, but clearly he could not hear hers to him.

If it weren't for his voice raging through her head, she'd feel utterly alone.

Tears of frustration rolled down her cheeks. Her throat was sore and her voice hoarse from screaming. She didn't have time for this! Baby Lynn could die any day. And Pete! What would Mrs. Holt and Bobby think when they returned home and Pete wasn't back from the hospital, as Therese had promised? Would they get rid of the golden retriever?

She screamed again. "Let me out of here!" Her throat stung with pain. "Let me out of here!"

Feeling along the floor with her hands, she recognized fine sand mixed with pebbles. She scooted on her hands and bottom, trying to get a sense for how large a space her prison was. As she scooted along, her hands fumbled against a larger rock with a sharp point. Hopeful, she snatched it up and rubbed the point against the binding at her wrists, over and over, sawing as fast as she could, approaching the speed of light and creating so much heat she nearly produced a flame. At last, the binding broke and her arms were freed. She removed her blindfold and looked around.

"What on earth?"

She found herself in a pit about ten feet deep and twelve feet in diameter. The walls of the pit were made of smooth incandescent stone, which cast a purplish glow throughout the prison and emanated a low buzzing sound reminding her of the extra freezer back home in the basement. Above was an opening, three feet in diameter with a metal grate over it, also aglow.

"Hello!" She called out toward the opening. "Anyone there?"

When no one answered, she felt along the incandescent walls, hoping to find a hidden door. The walls seared her hands. "Ouch!" Fanning her burnt hands in the air, she studied the walls, finding the bright glow wasn't too hard on her eyes, but there was no crack or crevice, no hidden door.

The floor! She crouched on her hands and knees, her black jeans and top nearly white now from the dust, examining every inch of the dirt and pebble-covered ground, hoping for a trap door. Unlike the smooth walls, the ground did not emanate heat or purple light. She found her collapsible bow and slung it over her shoulder with her quiver. Then she had the idea of shooting an arrow through the opening, to see if anything would happen. She fitted the arrow and released it perfectly. It incinerated as soon as it broached the grate.

Discouraged but not without hope, she retrieved her sharp-pointed rock and struck the ground with it, her burnt hand, nearly healed, stinging from the contact. In spite of the pain, she found she could dig a hole in seconds with her godly strength. Full of renewed hope, she eagerly crawled next to the wall and started digging with the idea that she would tunnel below the incandescent wall, behind it, and up toward the surface.

Perhaps it was because her mind was so singularly focused, but however it happened, as she dug beneath the incandescent wall, she realized how she would get Callisto from the sky without upsetting the universe. She would find another bear to take her place. If she could switch the bears at the speed of light, she might be able to avoid any repercussions to both the universe and the notice of humankind. She didn't know exactly how the bear held the stars, light-years away from one another, together in their constellation, but if one bear could do it, another could. She would see to it, but she needed a bear. There were plenty in the woods near her house.

She didn't want to force one against its will. That would make her no better than the other gods who used people and animals for their own selfish purposes. No, she had to find a way to convince a bear to volunteer. First, she had to get out of this pit.

She hadn't yet decided whether she would feed the apple to Pete or return it to Hera. If she fed it to Pete, she would likely lose Hera's favor forever, and worse, Baby Lynn would die. But she remembered reading that Artemis, too, was sometimes called upon to help the unborn because immediately after her own birth, she helped her mother travel to a safer island away from Hera's wrath to give birth to Apollo. Maybe Therese could feed the apple to Pete and then ask Artemis to save Lynn. A shiver worked its way down her spine as she realized she had nothing to give the goddess of the hunt in exchange for the favor. Could Artemis be trusted to give another gift out of the kindness of her heart? The goddess was generous to Therese when she was human, but things seemed different between them now.

Therese could return the apple to Hera, and then ask her to save both Lynn and Pete. She bashed the rock against the earth, again and again, frustrated by the thought that, Hera, too, would have no reason to help her beyond her original promise.

Although she had successfully dug beneath the incandescent wall, she hadn't made much progress tunneling up toward the surface when something fell from the opening above with a thud. Turning, she saw it was a man. He held a spear in his hands and wore torn trousers and no shirt on his muscled torso. His sky blue eyes glared at her warily through

145

blond messy bangs, and his strong jaw lifted in defiance as he climbed to his feet and crouched with the spear pointed at her.

"Who are you?" She stood up and backed away.

"Leif Anders, from Norway. Who are you?"

"You don't know? I thought I was your prisoner."

"Am I not yours?" Leif looked to be in his early twenties and was tall, broad, and strong, but was clearly just a man. Despite his size and weight, she felt confident she could defend herself against him if he attacked.

"You're the one with the spear."

He narrowed his eyes, as though he didn't trust her. "It's hard to see you in this purple haze."

"I'm Therese Mills from the U.S. Where are we?"

"Amazon territory."

"The rainforest?"

He shook his head. "I don't know our exact location. It's kept secret. You don't want to know either. I've heard they kill anyone who discovers it."

"They?"

"The Amazons."

"What? The Amazons? Why?" She paced around him, and he turned defensively with his spear keeping himself square to her. "What would the Amazons want with me?"

"To reproduce for them. That's what they want with me. If it's a girl, they let us go. If it's a boy, they kill him and make us start again."

Her jaw dropped open. "What?"

"They're a tribe of women. They capture men for reproduction."

"They can't find anyone willing?"

"What man wants his son murdered? And it's not like the Amazons are desirable. Their faces are beautiful, but they cauterize their right breasts as infants."

"What? Why would any woman mutilate her young like that?"

"They believe it makes them better warriors with the spear."

"That's so…antiquated and morbid, especially when we have automatic assault weapons."

"They're loyal to their traditions. Another reason why I'm here instead of a sample from a sperm bank."

"So they're really going to force you to have sex with them?"

"That's what they said just before they tossed me down here. I think I'm meant to have sex with you."

The blood rushed to her face. "No. No, not me."

"So you aren't going to rape me?"

"God, no. I want to get us out of here." She crossed her arms at her chest, trying to think why the Amazons would take her prisoner. Then she remembered that the first Amazons were daughters of Ares. He must have solicited their help in keeping her away from Than. How ironic that Leif was here to be forced to reproduce while she was here to be kept from it—unless they meant for her to become impregnated by a man as a way to prevent her from conceiving a god's child. Was the god of war buying himself some time? Nine months to be exact? A demigod would be no threat to him if she was raised among the Amazons. Her heart sped up and pounded against her ribs as she returned to her digging. "I think I've found a way out."

He dropped his spear. "They'll kill us if we try to escape."

"We can't let them catch us then."

He surprised her from behind, shoving her to her bottom. "Stop digging! They'll kill us!"

She pushed him away, but not with her full strength so as not to hurt him. "It's okay. I'll protect you."

"*You'll* protect *me*? Yeah, right. Now let's get this over with. They won't bring us food or water till the deed is done."

He came at her again, and this time she forced him to the ground. "Give it up! I'm stronger than you."

"I didn't believe them when they told me you'd be." He took a vial from his trouser pocket and removed the cork. "Didn't drink their damn elixir, sure it was a sleeping potion." He swallowed its contents and tossed the vial to the ground. "Didn't quench my thirst, but they said it would give me strength. I'm so thirsty. I've been their prisoner for days without food or water. Now come on. Please. Let's get this over with. I promise to be gentle."

Chapter Twenty-Six: Interrogation with the Furies

"You have your methods," Tizzie growled at Than, her dark serpentine curls coming alive, like the hair of Medusa.

"And we have ours." Blood dripped from Meg's eyes as she bent over the former Queen of the Amazons.

"But she says she doesn't know where it is," Than objected. "This is a waste of time."

The two Furies had Hippolyta connected to their stretcher in the upper pit of Tartarus, not far from where Tantalus lay with water dripping on his forehead and grapes dangling just out of his reach. Even though Hippolyta was as transparent as all souls in the Underworld, her raven hair sparkled, as did the metal trim on her boots and armor. Her dark eyes were wide with fright and her teeth clenched with pain. Than fought the impulse to rescue her from his sisters, who were trying to help him.

Tizzie cranked the stretcher. "You'd be surprised what souls can remember with a little help from this machine."

Hippolyta shrieked. "I told you, I gave the girdle to Hercules!"

Meg leapt on top of the table, her blond hair flying like golden flames, the falcon on her shoulder, ready to peck. Meg straddled the Amazon, allowing the blood from her eyes to spill onto Hippolyta's face. "That's not what he says. He says he stole it from you and then gave it back, after his labor was complete."

Hippolyta pressed her mouth and eyes closed to avoid the blood and then screamed, "Liar!"

"Why aren't you interrogating Hercules?" Than insisted.

Tizzie cranked the stretcher. "He's next."

Hippolyta said in a frantic, pleading voice, "I gave it to Hercules! He wanted everyone to think he bested me, for the sake of his labor, but I fell in love with him and gave it to him as we sailed together to Athens. But, but then he betrayed me!" Tears flowed from the corners of her eyes and down to her ears.

"Betrayed you, how?" Meg demanded.

"Hera wanted him to fail," Hippolyta said through gritted teeth. "She spread a rumor that he abducted me. My sister Antiope believed it and led an army of Amazons to attack Athens. Hercules…" Hippolyta stopped, fighting off sobs.

"Speak!" Tizzie hissed, echoed by the serpent curls. "Speak!"

"Hercules gave me back, refused me!" Hippolyta said as she wept. "His men were more important to him!"

"And the girdle?" Meg demanded.

"I think Hercules gave it to Theseus, but I'm not certain."

"Aha!" Tizzie loosened the stretch machine and turned to Meg. "I'll fetch Theseus while you take her to Erebus to purge her pain."

"What about Hercules?" Than said. "I thought you said he was next."

"Come with me, brother," Tizzie said. "If you want him so badly, I'll let you interrogate him."

Unlike his former arrogant self, Hercules was docile where he sat in the Elysium Fields. He didn't resist when Than beckoned him to follow, but the moment he was strapped to the stretcher, he became aware. Pain was the great tool of awakening.

Tizzie strapped Theseus on a second machine so that the two fallen heroes lay side by side, their armor mirror reflections of each other. Only the color of their hair—Hercules blond and Theseus black—kept them distinct from a distance. Meg returned from Erebus and leapt onto Theseus, frightening him with the blood from her eyes and the falcon at her shoulders, threatening to peck his face.

Than bent over Hercules. "What do you know of Hippolyta's girdle?"

"I returned it to Hippolyta when I gave her back to the Amazons."

"Lies!" Tizzie hissed, and her serpent hair echoed. "Lies!"

In the distance, Tizzie's wolf howled while she cranked the stretcher.

Hercules grunted. "Theseus, old friend! I'm sorry!"

"So you did give the girdle to him!" Than said.

"No one was to know, but yes. Now get me down!" Hercules cried.

"Why was no one to know?" Than demanded. "Tell me!"

Tizzie pulled the crank as Meg brought her falcon down to Theseus's face.

"What became of Hippolyta's girdle!" Meg shrieked.

Hercules panted as sweat poured from his skin. "Tell them, Theseus!"

"I gave it to Antiope, to woo her!" Theseus cried with pain.

"Hippolyta's sister?" Than asked.

"She fell in love with me and turned against her own people after they attacked us. She fought alongside me and protected me from her own sisters."

"Keep going!" Meg prodded, blood dripping from her face to his throat.

"She believed me when I told her of Hera's lie, but she couldn't convince the other Amazons of our innocence, so she killed for me. But..."

"But what?" Than said, rushing to Theseus's side. "Get to the point!"

"When I gave the girdle to Antiope, she was horrified. She thought Hercules and I had killed Hippolyta, even though Hippolyta died at the hands of her own people. The Amazons didn't recognize her when they killed her."

"Did you tell Antiope this?" Meg asked.

"Of course, but she wouldn't believe me. She took her own life and broke my heart. I lied about her death in our treaty with the Amazons, claiming they had killed her along with her sister. I also lied about the girdle, worried they'd jump to the same conclusions as Antiope."

"What became of the girdle?" Than's urgent voice echoed throughout Tartarus.

"The sea nymph Dione promised me safe passage back to Athens if I gave it to her, so I did."

Than's mouth dropped open. "Dione?"

Theseus nodded.

"Are you speaking the truth?" Than asked.

Tizzie cranked the machine.

"I swear! I swear! I gave the golden girdle to Dione!"

Chapter Twenty-Seven: Tunnel Vision

"Leif! No!" Therese jumped to her feet and pushed against the Norwegian, but he clung to her.

He crushed her in his arms and kissed along her neck. "Can't we make this pleasant?" he murmured. "Mmm. You smell nice." He clutched her hair and lifted her face to his. "And fortunately for me, you're beautiful." He covered her mouth with gentle lips.

She spat at him. "I promised myself to someone else!"

He wiped his mouth on her black shirt, over her right breast.

"Stop!"

His sky blue eyes pleaded with her. "You'll never get out of here alive unless you bear them a girl. I've heard the stories. Please. Let's make the best of it." He kissed her again.

She bit down on his lip.

"Ah!" He loosened his hold on her.

She stepped back and kicked him in the chest. He staggered back.

"Fine!" He raised both hands in the air. "I give up. Dig your tunnel."

She watched him warily as she found her rock and returned to her digging. "Nothing against you. I'm in love with someone else. We're going to get married."

"Keep dreaming," the Norwegian said. "Even if you do tunnel all the way out, they'll only capture you again. This place is heavily guarded."

"I told you, I'll find a way."

For another hour, she worked, tunneling up the other side of the incandescent wall. The loose dirt and rock fell in her hair, mouth, and eyes, making her cough and spit and blink, but she kept going, desperate to escape. She resented the Norwegian, who'd made himself comfortable in the middle of the pit, lying on his back, sometimes watching her, sometimes closing his eyes. She could no longer see him now that she could stand on her feet and crouch in the three-foot tunnel she'd made. Every fifteen minutes or so, she had to stop digging to push the fallen debris into the pit and out of her way.

"Oh, Than," she prayed. "If only you could hear me."

"Therese?"

"Than? You can hear me?"

"Yes! But I can't sense you! Where are you?"

"I don't know! The Amazons have me in some kind of enchanted pit. I'm trying to dig myself out."

Before she could explain more, the Norwegian grabbed her by her sneakers and pulled her from her tunnel, her head and arms hitting and scraping against the rock. He tugged her into the middle of the pit and climbed on top of her.

"Worn out yet?" His body was flush on top of hers, but he lifted his head to look at her, elbows propped on the ground on either side of her. He pushed her hair out of her eyes. "I'm starving and dying of thirst down here. Forgive me for what I'm about to do."

He pinned her down with his body as he ripped open her black jeans and tugged them past her hips.

"Stop!" she screamed. "Please!"

When he lifted himself to undo his own trousers, she reached back for an arrow from her quiver and stabbed him in the chest. He immediately transformed into a yellow canary, fluttering above her.

"What's happened to me?" he chirped.

"I didn't know what else to do."

"Change me back!"

"I can't. I'm sorry."

"Then I'm getting out of here!" He flew toward the grate above them.

"No! You'll get fried!"

He ignored her and flew up. Like her arrow, as soon as he broached the grate, he disappeared in a puff of smoke.

"Leif!" Therese covered her face and wept. "I had no choice," she said again, this time to herself. "I had no choice."

A few minutes later, she wiped her eyes with the back of her hands, fastened her jeans back at her waist, and found her rock.

Then it came to her. It came so fast she squealed with surprise, clutching the locket near her throat. If Than could hear her prayers while she was in the tunnel, maybe she could god travel, too. With her bow and quiver slung over her shoulder, she crawled beneath the incandescent wall and into the three-foot tunnel she'd made on the other side. As soon as she focused on Than's chambers, she was there, safe in his room. Hades appeared a moment later.

"Well played," he said.

"You knew where I was?" Therese asked with astonishment.

"Not in time to do anything about it." Hades scratched his beard. "The Amazonian Pit is the only territory underground I cannot control. Even Poseidon's sea caves are subject to me and my power." He narrowed his eyes. "Are you hurt?"

She shook her head. "I'm fine. Where's Than?"

"He must be well distracted not to sense your presence here." He crossed the room and sat in one of the club chairs in front of the fireplace, crackling with flames and wood.

"I thought he'd be here."

"He's in Tartarus, among other places, torturing souls." He steepled his fingers and smiled, as though delighted by the idea.

"What?"

"He needs information to help you."

"Never mind. He can't come with me, anyway. I need to go."

"Go? Where?"

"On a quest."

He motioned for her to sit in the chair opposite him.

"I don't have time. My sister's life is in jeopardy. Artemis gave me a quest in exchange for her help."

"What would the huntress have you do?"

"It's a secret."

"Ah, a secret quest. Wonderful. As soon as you leave my kingdom, Ares will hurl you back into the Amazonian Pit. This time, free of sharp rocks for digging."

She sank into the chair opposite him. "What can I do to protect myself? Artemis made it very clear that I can't involve Than."

"Hmm." He tugged at his beard. "Take the Furies with you."

"Thanks, but I promised I would go alone."

"Alone? With Ares after you? Impossible."

"I have to try." She stood up to leave.

"Then wear this." Something appeared in Hades's hand. A golden helmet? "My helm of invisibility."

"But…"

"Even the gods can't sense you while you're wearing it."

She sat back down on the edge of her chair. "Are you serious?"

"Quite. Though Zeus and Poseidon can sometimes become suspicious if you travel by sky or sea." He brought the helm to his face to inspect it carefully. "I've never been able to figure out what gives me away to them." He stood up and took her hand, helping her to her feet. "In any case, if you stick to the land, you'll be safe."

The sky and the sea were the two places she *must* go to complete her quest. She hid her fear and gave Hades a grateful smile.

Hades added, "And don't god travel. The helm won't protect you if you do. Now, come. I'll take you home in my chariot. Persephone's home. She can mind the store."

"I don't know how to thank you." She followed him from the room, presumably toward the garage.

"Oh, don't worry," he said, turning back to her with an unnerving smile. "I'm sure I'll think of a way."

Chapter Twenty-Eight: A Bear in the Woods

Wearing Hades's helm of invisibility, which wobbled uncomfortably, being a bit large for her head, Therese checked in on Carol and Richard to find Richard on the deck feverishly typing on his laptop and Carol eating a bowl of soup in front of the television, sobbing to some soap opera, rubbing her swollen belly. Therese couldn't tell if it was the knowledge that the baby was dying or the drama on the television or both that was making her weep. She wondered for a moment what it must feel like, carrying a baby you could not protect, knowing your own body was killing her. Hope kept Carol from terminating the pregnancy. Although the doctor warned her that she would likely have to suffer through a stillborn birth, Carol hoped he was wrong.

Therese took consolation in the fact that neither was concerned with her whereabouts, even though she'd been gone for seven hours. Given the note she left them on the bar, they must think she was at Jen's.

Not that the chariot ride with Hades had taken much time. Swift and Sure flew from a chasm of the Underworld and up into the bright afternoon skies of Colorado faster than Therese could swallow. At least she didn't have the burden of making small talk.

Next, she checked in on the Holts. Their trail ride season had ended the weekend after Labor Day, and today was the end of September, but the horses still had to be exercised on Saturday and Sunday now that Jen and Bobby were back at school during the week. Nevertheless, Therese was surprised to see Jen and Bobby riding even though Pete was missing. He wasn't missing, of course, for Therese saw him, still in the form of a golden retriever, sitting forlornly by the pasture gate licking his wound and waiting for Jen to return. Therese entered the house under the helm of invisibility to find Mrs. Holt on the phone, a pen and a cigarette in each hand, and a list of nearby hospitals written on a pad at her elbow. All but three were crossed out.

"Can I leave my number in case he's there and you just don't know it?" Mrs. Holt said into the phone.

Therese watched on, feeling terrible, as Mrs. Holt relayed her contact information to the woman on the other end. Mrs. Holt then hung up, sucked at her cigarette, and ran her hand through her gray-blonde, bowl-cut hair.

"Maybe I should try Therese again." She punched the numbers on her phone. "Maybe this time someone will answer."

What? Therese pulled at her hands, trying to think of what to do. If Mrs. Holt called her aunt and uncle, they would know she was missing and become concerned. What to do? What to do?

"Hello, Carol?" Mrs. Holt said. "I'm sorry to bother you, but I was wondering if I could speak with Therese."

Therese stepped outside through the exterior wall, removed her helmet, and knocked on the back door before entering. "Mrs. Holt? Jen asked me to...oh, sorry. Didn't know you were on the phone."

"Never mind, Carol. Therese is here. Sorry. Yeah, I didn't realize. Thanks anyway. I'll tell her." She hung up the phone and looked at Therese. "Thanks for all the work you did for us in the barn and with the horses this morning. That must have taken you hours."

"Not really."

"I didn't realize you were still here. I'm going crazy trying to find Pete. What hospital did the ambulance take him to?"

"Um, gosh, they didn't say. But I bet he's left by now. The cut wasn't *that* bad. I think the blood just freaked us all out. You know Jen."

"I've called a dozen different places and none of them claim to have seen him. And he's not answering his cell phone."

159

Therese knew the longer she went without the helm, the more vulnerable she'd be to Ares finding her.

"What's that in your hand?" Mrs. Holt asked.

"Oh, um, this?" What could she say? "This is part of a costume, for larping. You know, live action role play? Heard of it?"

Mrs. Holt shook her head and stood from the kitchen chair. "No, but I better get to work. Maybe you're right and Pete called a friend to come get him. Maybe he's milking his wound to get out of working today."

"Maybe." She headed for the back door. "Listen, would you mind if the golden retriever hangs out here for a while until I find him a home? Pretty please?"

"Oh, sure. One more animal won't make a difference on this ranch. I like him. He's fond of Jen, isn't he? Maybe we'll keep him."

Great. Therese gave Mrs. Holt a forced smile. "Well, I have to um, join Jen." She needed Mrs. Holt to think she was hanging out at their ranch in case Carol called.

"Sure thing." Then she added, "Didn't you say Jen wanted you to tell me something?"

"Oh." Therese stopped at the back door, hand on the knob. "I can't remember what it was. Sorry." She bolted out, put on the helmet, and ran back to her own house, to the woods behind it.

Once she caught her breath, she reached out her consciousness to sense the beings inhabiting the national forest up the mountain. "Than?" she felt him nearby.

"Where are you?" he prayed.

"In the forest. Where are you?"

"What a relief! In your room. I can't sense you."

"I'm wearing your father's helm." She jogged down the path toward her house.

160

"Really? He never lets anyone borrow it."

"Meet me on the back deck."

"Okay. But watch out for your uncle."

"I see him."

When she spotted Than, she threw her arms around his neck. "Thank God!"

He reached for her, but his arms moved through her. "I can't feel you. I can't sense you at all. I can only hear your prayer."

She removed the helm for just a moment and pressed her lips to his. They both remained invisible to mortal eyes, their words inaudible to mortal ears, which was necessary since her uncle was typing on his laptop less than twenty feet away.

"Mmm. Thank goodness," he moaned, pulling her close against him.

She kissed him back, but quickly returned the helm. "I've got to go."

"Where?"

"Artemis's quest. I promised her I'd keep it a secret. It's the only way she'll help me."

"I don't like this. Take me with you."

"Goodbye, Than." She backed away from him.

"Wait! Therese! Please! I want to protect you! Come back!"

She ran up the path despite his pleas for her to return, blocking his prayers as best she could as she wiped the tears from her cheeks and scrambled toward the top of the mountain, where she could sense the bears.

It felt cruel, leaving Than like this, but she had no choice. Lynn's life—and Pete's—hung in the balance. For now, getting the apple from Artemis seemed her only hope of saving either of them. Than would

161

understand, but that didn't mean her heart wasn't aching to have him by her side.

It wasn't long before she saw them—a mother and two cubs. The cubs were walking toward her across a log ten yards away while the mother looked warily from the mouth of a cave partially shrouded by chokecherry bushes. The mother lifted her black head and snorted.

Although Therese was a god and completely invisible, old habit made her tremble with mortal fear. She slowly backed away.

The mother bear took three strides from her den and called to her cubs, as though she sensed Therese's presence.

The cubs were older, and would probably go on their own in the spring, but Therese needed a bear that could leave now. This mother bear was not for her. She turned and ran around to the other side of the mountain.

She sensed other mothers with their cubs and a few solitary males, but none she thought would be willing to spend eternity in the sky. She kept searching, feeling frantic and foolish. What was she thinking, running around the mountainside? Was she crazy?

The warm scent of pine lingered in the forest air as the gray clouds gathered above for their typical afternoon shower. Birds sang or cried. Chipmunks jumped from tree to tree.

Further up the mountain, she sensed an old female bear, alone, fishing in the spring that fed into the Holts' pasture miles below. Less agile, less quick, and with patches of fur missing along her back and flanks, this bear was exactly what Therese was looking for.

"Hello!" Therese called out to her from ten feet away.

The bear turned in Therese's direction, and, seeing and hearing nothing, resumed her fishing in the stream.

"How would you like to live forever?"

The bear moaned something incoherent and trudged further up the stream.

As Therese was about to speak again, the old bear growled and ran toward a young female fishing several yards away.

"My territory!" the old bear roared.

"Huh?" came a snort of surprise from the younger female. When she saw the old bear running toward her, she wailed, "Wait! My mother drove me away. I have no place to go!"

The old bear hurled herself at the younger. "Leave!"

A cacophony of growling followed, along with threatening looks and gestures from both bears. Therese stood still, wondering how she could grab the old bear and carry her off.

Before Therese could intervene, the older bear struck the younger, and as the two bears fell against the banks of the stream, Therese heard the snap of the brittle spine of the old female, and then its body lay limp on the wet rocks.

"No!" If only Therese had been quicker. She ran to the side of the unmoving bulk on the bank as the younger bear moved away, downstream. Therese lifted the old bear's head and gently stroked its mouth as it panted and moaned. "You're alive. I may be able to save you. Tell me, old bear. Do you want to live forever in the sky?"

Chapter Twenty-Nine: Dione Revisited

While Meg and Tizzie escorted the two demigods to Erebus, Than communicated his new knowledge to Athena and Hephaestus, who'd been flying above the seas combing their depths for the lost girdle. He also shared Dione's earlier deception and his bewilderment over her motive. The three gods met on the northern shore of Turkey, at the banks of the Black Sea, where Than last spoke to the deceitful Oceanid.

"Therese escaped," Than said. "I just spoke to her. But until we find that girdle, I fear for her safety."

"Surely she's safe in the Underworld," said Athena.

Than frowned. "She's off on a quest for Artemis, hoping to save her sister's life."

"Honorable but foolish under these circumstances." Hephaestus scooped up a handful of sand and carefully sifted through it.

"Hades gave her his helm." Than turned to face the breeze off the water. It felt good after so much stress, but there was no time to rest.

Athena arched a brow. "He must like her a great deal."

"I sense Dione nearby." Hephaestus clapped his hands together to clean them of sand. "I think I know why she deceived you."

"Is that so, Hephaestus?" Dione's silver hair and eyes shimmered in the foam clinging to the rocks at their feet.

"You are my mother-in-law, after all," the god of the forge replied. "I've loved you more than I do my own mother."

Dione smiled. "Then you understand why I've hidden Ares's monstrous contraption?"

So she admitted it, Than thought.

"I still recall the day you asked me to make its opposite for your daughter."

"You're a good god, Hephaestus. A good husband to have done so, even at the cost of your own happiness. Passions of the heart are meant to be fed, not stifled."

"Passions are best subdued." Athena widened her stance and lifted her chin defiantly. "I'm afraid we have different philosophies, Dione."

Than was about to move the focus back to saving Therese, when Dione replied, "Indeed, virgin goddess. You, Hestia, and Artemis see the purpose of existence quite differently than I."

"Don't put me in the same category as Artemis. Her passions are tempered only by the absence of her heart's true love."

"Who's that?" Than asked, wondering if the answer might be related to Therese's quest.

"Callisto, of course," Athena replied. "Big Bear."

Than absorbed and processed Athena's words. What quest could have anything to do with Callisto?

"But you remain chaste by your own free choice," Dione objected. "Hippolyta's golden girdle offers no freedom. Once it's fitted, a woman is held prisoner by it. No woman should give up the rights to her own body."

"Agreed." Than stepped closer to Dione and gazed down at her. "But the girdle can be fitted temporarily, can it not? Hippolyta had the power to remove it and give it to Hercules."

"Yes," Dione agreed. "But if you expect Ares to leave Therese alone, he will want to fit it to her himself. Then only he can remove it."

Than looked up at Athena and Hephaestus, but they made no comment. "Until Therese and I can find a better way to protect ourselves from Ares, the golden girdle is our best solution."

"A temporary solution, Mother," Hephaestus echoed.

Dione scoffed. "What makes you so certain Ares will ever agree to remove it once he's fitted it to her?"

"Everyone wants something," Than replied. "I just need to find out what Ares wants, more than our chastity."

"And you can't keep her in the Underworld under your father's protection?"

"That would be another kind of prison," Than replied. "She needs to be able to visit her family." He didn't want her to be trapped in the Underworld. He wanted her to be free. "Plus, she's the goddess of animal companions and wouldn't be able to serve from the Underworld. Her transformation wouldn't hold in that case."

"If I hand over Hippolyta's girdle, what shall I get in return? One of you will owe me. And the girdle must be returned to me the moment Therese no longer requires it."

The other two gods on the bank stared at Than, waiting for his reply.

Chapter Thirty: Out in the Open Sea

Therese crouched on the bank of the stream with the old bear's head in her hands. If Than came to collect the bear's soul, neither he nor Therese could do anything to prevent the bear from dying. Her powers as goddess of animal companions did not extend to healing. If they did, she would have been able to heal Pete once he transformed into a golden retriever.

She wondered if she could ask Than to hold off taking the bear's soul, to give Therese time, but then she would have to betray her promise to Artemis.

As goddess of wild animals and as one of the Olympians, Artemis did have the power to save the old bear's life, but Therese worried Artemis might take the bear and complete the quest on her own, keep the apple, and leave Therese with no leverage to seek Hera's aid in saving Lynn.

Therese had to do this on her own if she had any hope of saving Lynn and Pete, though she still had no idea how she would save both. Her face flushed as she realized she was putting her own needs ahead of those of the old bear.

I'm exactly like the other gods.

Not wanting to waste another moment, Therese grabbed the bear's front legs, and hefted the furry beast onto her back, careful to shift the quiver of arrows to one side. The bear moaned in protest.

"I'm going to help you," Therese assured her. "Just hold on a while longer." She hesitated, wondering if she should let the old bear die and find a younger, stronger bear for her journey, like the younger bear downstream, but the younger bear had her whole life ahead of her, and flinging her into the sky for all eternity might seem more a punishment to her. This bear would die otherwise; plus, Therese didn't want to waste any more time.

Without god travel or a chariot, she had no choice but to traverse land and water in what her senses told her was a bee-line to the Aegean Sea, where Artemis said Big Bear's feet touched the horizon at night. She was tempted to take her chances and god travel, but if Ares caught her again, she'd never save Lynn and Pete. So, with the helm of invisibility on her head, her quiver and bow over her left shoulder, and the old bear slumped across her back, its back paws almost grazing the ground, Therese clung to the bear's forelegs at her neck and ran down the mountainside as fast as she could manage. She ran through the San Juan Mountains and National Forest past the Great Sand Dunes, and over the last of the Rocky Mountains, moving southeast across grassland into Kansas. It took an hour to reach the river, where she laid the bear down to rest, giving her water and consoling her as best she could. Above her, in the late afternoon sky, buzzards swirled over them, sensing the old bear's demise, so she put her hands on the bear again to extend the helm's powers to her, and the vultures eventually flew away.

Then she followed the Cimarron National Grasslands northeast into Missouri, avoiding heavily populated cities as much as possible—not because she or the bear could be seen, since everything she touched was also protected by the helm, but because the city landscape slowed her down. In some areas, she risked being sensed by Zeus and took flight, but only when it was unavoidable. At one point, when she was flying into the Ozarks over Branson, a flock of geese followed her, and it felt more than coincidental. Therese worried they were working for Zeus. When she veered to her left, so did they. When she veered to the right, they followed. Trying not to panic, she landed near a lake in the Ozarks and decided to stick to the ground from then on.

She found her way through the Ozarks, stopping briefly in the Bald Knob Wilderness of southern Illinois to catch her breath and give water to the bear. She used a clam shell to scoop water from the river and drizzle it into the panting bear's mouth. In another hour, dusk would come, but the bear would not survive if Therese didn't give her opportunities to rest. She dipped the clam into the river, when suddenly a water moccasin sunk its fangs into the top of her hand. Painful poison surged through her veins. She pulled her hand away and dragged the bear from the bank, sure Poseidon or another sea deity must recognize her presence. She decided she would continue to follow the river but would be more careful about touching it for the rest of her journey.

Without stopping, she trailed the Ohio River along the Indiana and Ohio borders, and then crossed through the Glades of West Virginia to the Virginia coast.

She was a god and was strong, but not invincible. Her hand and arms still burned from the snake's venom, and her feet, knees, and back ached, but she trod on. The old bear looked as though she might expire at any moment. Night was falling, and because she was moving east, she was losing time. To make matter worse, she had to find a way across the Atlantic and the Mediterranean to the Aegean Sea without losing the bear and without being discovered by Poseidon. If a deity had sensed her near the river in a small patch of land in Illinois, it would have a field day with her swimming, without an escape route, in the middle of the wide open sea.

"No more," the bear moaned as Therese looked out across the Atlantic, deciding on her next move. "I can't take anymore."

"Hold on," Therese urged. "Wouldn't you like to live forever in the sky?"

"And never die?"

"That's right."

169

"You can…really make that…happen?"

"If you want me to."

The bear panted a barely audible, "Yes," before passing out and losing consciousness.

"No!"

Therese pressed her hand against the old bear's chest and felt a fragile heartbeat and wondered if Lynn's heartbeat was also weak. What if Therese was too late? She bit her lip, wiped her eyes, heaved the beast onto her back, and dove into the sea.

She was able to help the bear to breathe and remain somewhat warm underwater. Because she had to use her hands to hold the bear's forelegs around her neck, Therese had no choice but to rely on her legs, and this slowed her down. She alternated between using the dolphin kick, breast kick, and flutter until she found the dolphin kick was the most efficient. She thought, mockingly, *Mental note: if you ever have to swim across the ocean with a bear on your back, the dolphin kick is best.*

She hadn't been in the water long when a school of sharks surrounded her. There were six of them circling her not ten feet away, baring their teeth. One by one, she shot them with her arrows, and as soon as they were pierced, they sidled up to her and nuzzled her hand. She asked them if they would escort her through the sea. The biggest and strongest offered her his back, but as she climbed on, holding the bear with one hand, a golden net fell over her, cinched her and the bear into a heap, and dragged them down, down, to the darkest depths of the sea.

Therese wrapped her arms around the bear, trying with all her might to keep the beast as comfortable as possible as they were mercilessly dragged through all manner of sea life and over rocky landforms, bouncing around as if they were tied to a trailer hitch and were being dragged through the Rocky Mountains by an SUV with four-wheel drive. Therese used her own body to shelter the blows to the bear, encasing the bear like the yolk of an egg. Her skin stung where coral, rock, and shell dug into her as she passed. Both fear and relief came over her when the brightly lit palace that belonged to Poseidon came into view.

The net stopped in the middle of a courtyard just outside of the palace walls. Poseidon swam toward them with his trident, and in a booming voice that blasted her eardrums like an IPod turned up to full volume, Poseidon demanded, "You thought you could sneak around my domain unnoticed? Exactly what is the meaning of this? Show yourself, Hades!"

Therese removed the helm to expose both herself and the bear, still in the net, floating but tethered.

"Therese?" Poseidon asked, sounding genuinely surprised. "It's you."

"I'm sorry I tried to be sneaky," Therese said. "I'm on a secret quest for Artemis."

"Why must you travel through my domain for Artemis?"

"It has nothing to do with your domain. I promise. I'm just passing through."

"It's hard to trust an oath breaker."

"Please let me pass. I'll do anything you ask."

The golden net disappeared and a group of merfolk swam to the aid of both Therese and the bear, keeping them from floating away while guiding them toward Poseidon. The bear was still unconscious, its tongue hanging from its mouth, its eyes closed, and its heart barely beating. The school of sharks remained faithfully behind, wagging their tales like dogs.

"I'm running out of time, Poseidon. If I don't finish my quest. before this bear dies, I won't be able to save my baby sister or my friend."

"I can't afford to have Ares against me," Poseidon said. "You must understand how complicated the relationships between the gods can be."

"I'm getting the idea."

Poseidon placed his trident on the bear's back, and a bright light emanated from its prongs and over the bear and throughout the water in rings that lit the sea for miles. "I just bought you some time. Now come inside and tell me why I should let you cross."

Therese was pleased to see the bear open her eyes. But once the old animal saw she was underwater among gods and merfolk, she flailed her legs in a panic and fainted with confusion. The fact that her heart beat strong and steadily was reassuring to Therese, but this feeling did not last, for when she entered the palace doors, the god of war was there to greet her.

Chapter Thirty-One: Hippolyta's Golden Girdle

The golden girdle had not been in Than's possession long when Hermes arrived at his chambers in the Underworld to summon him to Poseidon's palace.

"What's this about?" Than asked.

"Ares has Therese. Everything's in chaos. If you come now, you can keep Therese from the Amazonian Pit."

"Ares has Therese?" He grabbed the golden girdle from his sideboard and followed Hermes.

Together they god traveled directly to Poseidon's palace, where Poseidon was on one side of the large foyer with Therese, a sleeping bear, eight merfolk, and a school of happy sharks. Ares was on the other side red-faced and yelling, his voice so much louder underwater than on land.

"Enough trifling!" Ares growled. "Hand her over!"

"Enough indeed!" Than tossed Hippolyta's girdle through the water to Ares, who caught it like a Frisbee. "This should lay your fears to rest!" Then he mumbled, "Along with my dreams."

Than prayed to Therese and made eye contact with her, "Are you okay?"

"I'm running out of time," she prayed back.

Ares inspected the belt with a smile. "Yes, Thanatos. I haven't seen this for centuries. Where did you find it?"

"Does it matter?" Than spat. "You have it now and should have no more reason to whine and moan about my future marriage."

"You agree to allow me to fit it to her?"

"Yes. I'd rather have her in chastity than not at all. Though it seems perfect bliss is a faraway dream."

"I learned that lesson years ago," said Ares. "The day Aphrodite was given to Hephaestus."

Than pounded his fist into his hand. "One day, I'll find a way to make you remove that girdle from Therese, and then our love and happiness will finally be complete."

"Good luck with that," Ares mocked.

"I'm a patient god." Than moved close to the god of war. "I will find your weakness, and I will exploit it until you have no choice. That's a promise."

"We shall see," Ares scoffed. "Meanwhile, let's get this over with. Poseidon?"

Poseidon moved away from Therese, but to Than's surprise, Therese did not look happy.

"Are you pleased with yourselves for having so happily determined my fate?" she snapped. "Well, I am not a child. I'm a god, like you, and I determine my own destiny, and I will not allow anyone to tell me what I can and cannot do with my own body!"

Before Than, or anyone, could reply, Therese was surrounded by a school of sharks, and with them and the sleeping bear, she god traveled from the palace. Ares looked about to follow, but Dione appeared in her full glory, large and beautiful with silver eyes and hair shimmering in the glow of her skin. She occupied most of the foyer, pressing against all present. In her sing-song voice, she said, "That's my girl! My own descendant! I couldn't be more proud! God of war, just try to interfere, just try to get past me, and I will suck you down into the darkest, deepest abyss beneath the sea!" She turned to Poseidon. "Will you fight me?"

"This is not my fight," Poseidon replied.

Dione then turned back to Ares. "If you want Aphrodite to continue to have anything to do with you, give me back that golden girdle!"

Than turned to Ares and was amused by the sight of the war god's mouth hanging so wide open that a minnow could find a comfortable home inside.

Chapter Thirty-Two: Betrayal

In the dark of night, Therese and her entourage of sharks arrived with the bear on the surface of the Aegean Sea beneath a blanket of stars. Therese combed the sky for the Big Dipper, and once she recognized its shape, was able to trace the Ursa Major constellation down to Big Bear's paws.

"Therese, talk to me," Than prayed.

"Let me finish this quest."

"Are you angry with me?" he asked.

She hadn't liked the way he'd assumed she would wear the girdle, but she knew he was trying to protect her. "We'll talk when I'm done."

"Okay." She could hear the hurt in his voice. "Be safe."

Oh, Than. She didn't want him to feel hurt. She couldn't wait to return to his arms. "I love you. I'll come to your rooms when I'm done."

"I'll be waiting."

She knew what she was about to do shouldn't be possible, but she closed her eyes and believed. Balanced on the backs of two sharks so as to avoid being detected by Zeus in the sky, she reached her hand up until she felt the palpable fur of a foreleg. Then, as she heaved the Big Bear down from the sky she hefted her old bear up in one counter-clockwise motion.

"Good-bye, old bear! I hope you enjoy your view of the world!"

"Thank you!" the old bear said.

Big Bear, larger and more powerful than the old bear, fell on Therese, plunging them both into the water. The sharks, unsure how to serve Therese, scattered but circled nervously around them. Therese bid them farewell as, gripping the bear, she god traveled back to the woods behind her home in Colorado, where the sun was just now beginning to set.

She hadn't yet removed her helm when Callisto asked, "What's happening to me?"

Therese showed herself, wet and coughing up sea water. When she could, she said, "My name is Therese. I'm the goddess of animal companions. Artemis asked me to reunite the two of you."

"Did it not occur to you to ask me what I wanted?" The bear stood up on her hind legs and stretched a foot taller than Therese.

Therese laced her hands together at her chest, feeling like the biggest hypocrite in the world. She had just yelled at a palace full of gods for making a decision on her behalf, and here she was doing the same thing to Callisto. Tears of frustration stung her eyes. "I'm sorry. I'll take you back."

Callisto came down on all fours. "No, I don't want to go back. I'm just angry at Artemis for not trusting me. I did nothing to deserve the punishment I served for so many centuries. It's hard to get over it."

Therese reached out with her hand, hesitant at first, but then continued when Callisto did not recoil or attack, and stroked the fur on the bear's back. Realizing this was not a gesture Therese would make if the bear were in her true form, she felt awkward and not sure at all how best to behave. "What do you want to do?"

"It's crazy, but I still love Artemis," she said. "Her prayers to me all these years have made life bearable. Where is she?"

"I am here," Artemis said from a shimmering cypress. She leapt from the tree and threw her arms around the bear's neck. Her voice cracked from the tears caught in her throat. "I never thought this day would come! I can't believe you're in my arms! Is this really happening?"

"I wish I could hold you properly," Callisto said. "A bear's body is so clumsy."

"I have a way to change you back." Artemis made the golden apple appear in her hand. "Eat this, and then we can be as we once were."

Trembling with disbelief over this betrayal, Therese fitted an arrow to her bow. "Stop! You promised that apple to me! I need it to save my sister!"

Artemis turned to face Therese. "I'm sorry, but this is the only way we can be together."

"But you promised!"

"Didn't Than break an oath to all of the gods of Mount Olympus so that he could be with you? And he swore on the River Styx."

"Artemis, please!" Therese cried.

"You don't need this apple to save your unborn sister," Artemis said. "I can save her, and then both of us can be happy."

"But what will Hera do when I don't return her apple?"

"What she always does. Listen, Therese, you can never get on Hera's good side. Even if you were to return the apple to her, she might not save your sister. You didn't require her to swear on the River Styx."

Therese considered this for a moment. "Would it be possible to share the apple?"

"No. Once the apple is defiled by a single bite, it's drained of all its power." Artemis turned back to Callisto. "Now eat, Callisto, before anything happens to this apple."

Therese raised her bow again. "Wait! I can pierce her heart with an arrow of hate before she swallows. If you don't want that, I need you to promise on the River Styx to save my sister's life!" It was a bluff. She had no more arrows of hate from Cupid.

A moment of clarity helped Therese to see the similarity between this situation and the one in which Than was forced to swear never to turn her into a god. She realized in that moment that she would never succeed in freeing Than of his annual visit by the maenads.

"I swear on the River Styx," Artemis said.

Therese lowered her bow, and Artemis fed the golden apple to the bear. Within seconds of her first bite, Callisto transformed into a beautiful nymph, strong and tall like Artemis with black hair and black eyes and bronze skin that gleamed in the starlight. She was breathtaking.

The two goddesses embraced. Therese said her goodbyes and then god traveled to Than's chambers to return Hades's helm and to tell Than about her next quest. She had to face Ladon and the Hesperides again. It was the only way to save Pete.

Chapter Thirty-Three: Therese's Return

Than took Therese in his arms and held her. "Let me go with you this time. I can help."

"That would be so awesome!" She circled her arms around his neck.

He noticed streaks of red when she rested her arms on his shoulders. "Look at your skin."

"I got a little scraped when Poseidon dragged me along the ocean floor."

"He what?" Than couldn't imagine Poseidon being cruel for no apparent reason.

"He thought I was your father sneaking into his domain."

"Are you okay?" He scanned her all over. "Your jeans are ripped. Are your legs okay?" He opened the holes in the back of her jeans to inspect her legs. "Looks like you're healing quickly enough."

"Yeah. It stung pretty badly while it was happening, but I'm fine." She wrapped her arms around him once more. "I wish we could stay."

He kissed her. It wasn't nearly as long as he'd wished. "Then let's stay." He ran his hands through her hair. "It's curlier than usual. I like it."

"Sea water and no blow dryer." She immediately looked self-conscious as she combed through her red curls with her fingers.

He grabbed her wrists and returned her hands behind his neck. "You look beautiful. Now where were we?"

"Can I use your magic phone again?"

He lifted his brow.

"Carol and Richard and Mrs. Holt are probably worried about me and Pete. What am I gonna say?"

"Let's see. It's seven o'clock at night there. Can you say you and Pete went somewhere together?"

"Well, his truck is still at home. How did we get there?"

He couldn't resist saying, "God travel?"

"Yeah, right." She paced the room. "Wait. I'll say I asked his friend Eric to come pick me up to look for Pete and when we found him with some other friends, we all went to hang out." She started dialing. "I'll say we needed to talk, to get things cleared up between us."

"You don't have to tell me the details." He didn't like the images she was conjuring.

When she hung up, she had a smile on her face.

"So?" he asked.

"They both said they wish we would have called and to come home immediately."

"I don't understand. Then why the smile?"

"Carol said Lynn is moving around a lot, like a healthy baby."

The corners of his mouth stretched of their own accord. "Artemis has already made good on her promise." He took her hands in his and kissed her.

"I made a difference. I can't believe it." She spun around on one foot to rest in his arms again.

"So how are you going to get Pete home immediately?"

"I told them we'd already bought movie tickets and convinced them to let us come home by midnight."

"So you bought yourself more time."

"Would you give this back to your father for me, and tell him thank you?" She took the helm from the sideboard where she had laid it when she had first arrived and handed it over to Than.

"Don't you need it?"

"No. I'm tired of hiding from Ares. Plus, we're going to god travel, and this won't protect me anyway."

Than felt blood rush to his face. "What do you mean you're tired of hiding from Ares? You do realize he will capture you again, don't you? And this time, you won't escape."

"But…"

"Listen. I know you're a god now, too. You've reminded me many times. And I know you're powerful and determined. I know you can take care of yourself. But Ares isn't someone to be taken lightly. Of all the gods, he's the cruelest and the most exacting. Even my father has more mercy than Ares."

"Than, calm down."

"Calm down?" How could he possibly calm down? It was like she was looking to get caught again. "Do you want to go back to the Amazonian Pit?"

"Of course not. But I have an idea."

He crossed his arms at his chest. "Well? What is it?"

"I want to offer him a truce."

"Oh." His shoulders sagged and his throat constricted. "Then I guess that means you've decided to wear the girdle."

"No. I'll never wear that thing."

"I'm confused. What do you have to offer?"

"Well, since I've already pissed off Hera by failing to return the apple from Artemis, I may as well steal as many apples from her garden as I can."

He pressed his palms through the air. "Hold on. This does not sound good."

She put her hands on his hips and playfully shook him. "How many kids do you want to have?"

He jerked back his head. Hip once told him that the conversational style of females was very different from that of males, but this was the first time Therese had changed topics so quickly and radically. "Um, I'm not following you."

She laughed. "How many kids do you want to have? Take Ares out of the equation."

He tapped his chin with three fingers. "I suppose if Ares couldn't threaten to separate us for all eternity…, I would want two or three. And by the way, I had to promise Dione we would name a daughter after her."

"Okay. I like that name. So let's say two."

"Why are we talking about this right now? Isn't Pete's life hanging in the balance? I mean, I'm happy for us to stay here all night and dream of the future kids we'll never get to have, but I don't understand why you've had a change of heart."

"I haven't." Her smile was contagious.

Maybe his father had been right the time he said gods and men would never understand goddesses and women.

"Oh, Baby, listen." Her smile was even brighter, which made him happy and confused at once. "Ares is hung up about us having kids because he doesn't want the balance of power skewed against him. Right?"

"Right. So?"

"So, in addition to taking a golden apple from Hera's garden to transform Pete, I'm going to take two more and offer them to Ares."

"Hera won't like that."

"Who would you rather have against us, Hera or Ares?"

"Good point, but how will that keep Ares from being against us?"

"I'll tell Ares that for each child I bear, he should use an apple to create his own immortal ally, to keep the power among the gods balanced."

"And if we have more than two children?"

"We'll cross that bridge when we get there." Her faced turned a little red.

"What's wrong?"

"Nothing. It's just that…well…. Goddesses don't get pregnant every time they have sex, right? Otherwise Ares and Aphrodite would have a ton of kids."

Desire flared in Than's heart. Her blushing cheeks and the awkward way she lowered her eyes made him want to sweep her into his bed. "Right." He cleared his throat, feeling the blood rush to his face. His cheeks were probably as pink as hers. "When a god and a mortal get together, a pregnancy always results. Between two gods, it's less often, but one can't predict when it will happen. They say only the Fates know."

Therese's eyes widened with a spark that meant she had an idea.

Just what he needed: another idea. "What?" he asked warily.

"The Fates live here, in the Underworld, right?"

"Right."

"Are they related to you?"

"They're my great-aunts, but I rarely see them because they're heavily guarded. Especially since that one time Apollo got them drunk to help his friend Admetus. You remember, the story I told you about…"

"Yeah, I remember. He's the one that asked his wife to die in his place."

"Yeah. Anyway, I don't think I've even been to their chambers. Our paths usually cross out there."

"Out there?"

"When I'm collecting souls. See, they also have the power of disintegration."

"Why? Why would they need to be at more than one place at a time?"

"They visit each person on his or her seventh day, when they weave, measure, and cut out the thread of life for that person."

Therese put her fists on her hips. "I don't believe that they get to decide how people live their lives. People have free will. Your brother said so, too."

"That's true."

"Then how can the Fates already know what a person's going to do?"

Than sat in one of the leather chairs in front of the fireplace and beckoned Therese to his lap. "I'm going to give you an analogy."

"Like the shower head?"

"Yes. Like the shower head. But this time, imagine you go see a fortune teller, and she says your shoe lace is going to break. Then your shoe lace breaks later that day. Just because she foresaw it, doesn't mean she caused it. Understand?"

"So you're saying the Fates see what we are going to do with our lives, but we still have the power to make our lives what we want them to be?"

"Not complete power, not total freedom, but yes."

"Why not total freedom?"

"Well, you don't get to choose your parents or the other circumstances of your birth, like what economic class you're born into, religion, culture, and so forth. If you're born a king you are limited and free in different ways than if you're born a slave."

"Okay, I see. But within certain parameters, people are free to make their own destinies."

"Yes. Within limited parameters."

"So when can you take me to them?"

He seriously doubted it was possible. "Both gods and people have tried to manipulate the Fates. Like I said, they're heavily guarded."

"But if the Fates don't cause your destiny."

"Well, they do weave part of it. Those things outside of your control. And then the goddess of chance comes into play. But people, especially demigods, have come seeking my aunts under the misguided notion that the Fates can change anything. They can't. Once a thread is woven it's immutable."

"Immutable?"

"Can't be changed."

"But can't you just explain that we don't want to change anything? We just want to know how many kids we're going to have."

He shook his head. "Nothing good ever comes from knowing what the future holds."

"But our case is different." She jumped from his lap. "We need to know so we can get Ares to cooperate."

He crossed the room and grasped her shoulders, looking hard into her eyes. "And what if we don't like what we hear?"

"Like what? That we won't have any kids?"

He nodded, but he worried there could be other information they wouldn't want to know, like her being captured by Ares and kept for all eternity in the Amazonian Pit, Than helpless to save her.

"Well…, that would be disappointing…, but then we could tell Ares with confidence that he has nothing to worry about. Don't you get it?" She pulled away to pace around his room again. "If we can find out for sure how many kids we're going to have, even if it's none, we can bring back the right number of apples and have more credibility when we make our proposition to Ares."

"The Fates are never wrong."

"Exactly." She turned to him and put her hands on his chest. "So how can we arrange to meet with them tonight?"

186

Chapter Thirty-Four: The Fates

The chamber belonging to the Fates resembled a Las Vegas casino. It was alight with blinking colors from slot machines crammed together with archaic pinball machines along the Phlegethon, which also illuminated the room as it flowed in a circle around the perimeter of the cave through a haze of thick cigarette smoke. Two tables occupied the middle of the room. The bigger and more central was a roulette wheel that emanated a barely audible melody reminding Therese of circus music. On the right side of the roulette wheel was a much smaller table with three chairs and stacks of playing cards. Sitting in each chair was a petite wrinkled old lady holding a cigarette. They didn't look up from their cards when Than and Therese entered.

"Is it already time for their visit?" said one in a raspy, throaty voice as she picked up a card. Half of her gray hair sat in a bun on the crown of her head, and the other half lay in straight lines along her back and shoulders, across her pink velvet pantsuit. "Hit me one more time."

"Are you sure?" The sister dealing was plumper than the others but as small in stature and throaty in voice. Her gray hair was short and curly and she wore a bright blue shawl over a blue velvet dress.

"Of course not, but hit me anyway." She looked at the card. "Damn. I'm busted." She tossed the card on the table and took a drag from her cigarette.

"Hit me," said the third, who wore her white hair in a bob with bangs that curled under, reaching the top of her black-rimmed spectacles. She took the card from the dealing sister and turned all three cards over. "Twenty-one. I'm on a roll tonight."

"I think I'll hit the slots for a while," the one in the pink velvet pantsuit said.

Her sister, who wore a lavender jacket and a denim skirt, pointed to Therese. "But what about our guests, Clotho?"

"You deal with them," Clotho replied. "I need to be amazed."

"Do you want me to bring that magician from the fifth century in again?" the one who had dealt offered.

Clotho sat down before one of the blinking machines, her back to Therese and Than. "No thanks, Lachesis. He was a little too predictable for my taste." She pulled the lever.

Lachesis stacked the cards back into a full deck and said, without looking up, "You may as well have a seat." She pointed to her own as she left the table to spin the roulette wheel. "Call out a number between one and a hundred."

Therese, taking Clotho's seat, glanced at Than.

"Fifty," Than said.

The one in the lavender jacket, who was the only sister seated at the table, said, "Don't you remember? He doesn't get it right."

"I'd forgotten, Atropos. But thank you for spoiling it for me," Lachesis, the dealer, complained before returning to the table. "Please, honey, take my seat," she said to Than. "I'd ask you how you've been, but I already know. And I'd ask you why you're here, but I know that, too. I don't know how you feel, so, tell me, Thanatos, how are you feeling?"

"Anxious," Than replied. "I've witnessed only bad consequences when people seek answers from you. By the way, you know Therese. Therese, these are my great-aunts. Clotho, across the room, is the spinner. Lachesis here is the measurer. Atropos is the cutter."

"Nice to meet you," Therese said, repeating their names in her head so she wouldn't forget them: Clotho, Lachesis, and Atropos.

"I wish that were true," Lachesis said. "But it won't be nice, dearie."

"What do you mean?" Therese asked.

Atropos of the spectacles and lavender jacket blew cigarette smoke from her mouth. "Only that it's best not to know what lies ahead. But, despite this warning, you will still ask your question, so proceed."

"We wouldn't ask it if we could think of any other way to be together," Therese said.

"Blah, blah, blah," Clotho said in her pink pantsuit from across the room. "Just get on with it. Ask your question. I'm ready for a game of roulette."

"Why do you play if you already know the outcome?" Therese asked.

"It's your turn, Atropos," Clotho said. "I answered it the last time it was asked."

"But that was two centuries ago," Atropos complained.

"It still counts," Clotho said.

Atropos sighed. "The threads of gods are woven, but they are neither measured nor cut like they are for the mortals. The threads belonging to us three Fates remain unwoven, for the sake of our sanity. We do not know the details of our own futures."

"Except for those moments when we cross paths with others," Lachesis added. "Such as this visit. That's how Atropos knew what number you'd call out, Than, dearie."

Atropos exhaled more cigarette smoke and said, "We are weary of always knowing what was, what is, and what will be. These games of chance in isolation from others divert us from our otherwise dreary existence."

"But each time a new person is born, you weave, measure, and cut a new thread," Therese said. "Each one is different, right?"

Clotho waved her hand through the air. "There's nothing new under the stars, dearie. One person's life in a given culture and context is very much like another."

189

Lachesis came around the table next to Therese and put a wrinkled hand on her shoulder. "Occasionally someone different comes along, but it's quite rare. You, for example. Your thread was a delightful surprise."

Therese smiled. "Thank you."

Atropos looked at Therese over her spectacles and from beneath her curled white bangs. "That doesn't mean you'll like the answer to your question."

"Ask already," the impatient Clotho said again.

Therese glanced at Than, who appeared as nervous and worried as she felt. Why wouldn't she like the answer? "Okay. How many children will Than and I have?"

"Two, but none immortal," Atropos said.

"What does that mean?" Therese asked.

"Are you sure you want to ask more questions, dearie?" Lachesis asked.

"If I remember correctly," Atropos began. "They ask one more."

"Yes, you remember correctly." Therese climbed from her chair to stand beside Than. "What does that mean, none immortal?"

Atropos rolled her eyes. "I mean you produce *mortal* children."

"Don't ask more," Than cautioned Therese. "We have enough information to satisfy Ares."

"But…" Therese wanted a better explanation.

Than shook his head and gave her an urgent stare. "Let's go," he said. "Thanks for your help, ladies."

"Oh, good," Clotho said jumping from her seat. "Time for roulette."

"Yes, thank you," Therese added.

"Our pleasure." Lachesis gave her a friendly nod.

190

Clotho shook her head as she crossed the room toward the roulette wheel. "I knew she would ask it, but I still hoped she wouldn't. Why? Why do I bother?"

Therese and Than god traveled back to Than's room.

"We need to see Ares immediately," Than said. "This will put his fears to rest."

"But what does it mean, no immortal children?"

He took her in his arms. "I don't know. I don't want to know."

"But I do. What if I can't remain a god?"

"They said we have children together. There's no way I could sire children by you if you return to being a mortal."

"Unless for some reason you, too, become mortal."

Than pulled away and faced the fire crackling in his fireplace. "I knew we shouldn't have gone."

"But at least we'll get Ares off our backs." She went to him and hugged him from behind, burying her face in his strong back.

"Can you be happy with me, knowing what you know? Can you just let the future be and enjoy the present?"

She nodded against him. "Yes. I'll trust that whatever happens, as long as you and I are together, we'll be happy."

He turned around and kissed her. "Mmm. That's my girl. Now, we need to see Ares."

"How do we manage that? I don't know if they'll let us in at Mount Olympus."

"Hermes can arrange a meeting."

Chapter Thirty-Five: Conference in Paris

Than thanked Hermes for summoning the others, and then he and Therese god traveled from his chambers to Paris. He had asked Hermes to invite Apollo, so the god of truth could vouch for the veracity of Than's statements to Ares, and for Aphrodite, so her presence would put Ares in a good mood. Alecto would also be present, in case Ares tried anything, like abducting Therese again.

Aphrodite and Ares were already seated beside one another at the table on the patio of Café Moulan when Than and Therese arrived with Alecto on their heels. They had barely sat down when Apollo appeared and joined them beneath the striped umbrella that stood erect through the center of their table.

"Thank you for meeting us," Than said to the others.

Apollo eyed the snake around Alecto's neck with disdain, reminding Than how much the gods of Olympus were revolted by members of Than's family. Only Hip and Persephone seemed immune to the negative bias against which the other members of the Underworld suffered.

"Hermes said you had important news for me." Ares took a sip from his wine.

"Yes, and I've asked Apollo to come since he can recognize a lie when he hears it. I want you to know I speak the truth."

"And Alecto?" Aphrodite asked with a forced smile.

Than could see through her attempt to be polite, and his ears became hot with anger.

Alecto licked her lips in a way that resembled the darting tongue of her snake and said, "For moral support."

"Go on," Ares said.

Therese jumped into the conversation. "We went to see the Fates."

"Oh?" Ares asked. "And what did they have to say?"

Than could see the blood rush to Therese's face. She said, "They see no immortal children in our future."

"No immortal children?" Aphrodite asked.

Than cleared his throat. "For reasons we don't yet know, Therese and I have two mortal children. We share this information with you, Ares, hoping this will alleviate your need to sabotage our marriage."

"Indeed," the god of war replied. "This is good news."

Therese narrowed her eyes. "I'm glad you're satisfied. Now you can leave me alone."

After a suspicious glance toward Apollo, Ares said, "Yes, I can."

Aphrodite reached across the table and took Therese's hands in hers. "I'm so glad we have this chance to talk, Therese, because I've wanted to tell you how proud I am of you."

"Thank you," Therese said, her face turning from red to pink.

"Do you know how much of who you are comes from your godly family?"

Therese shook her head.

"Before you became like us, you already possessed gifts. You could fly in your dreams, and that helped you to control them. Your ability to fly with such zest comes from Zeus, whose blood runs in me, to Cupid, and down the line to you."

"I hadn't thought of that. I love to fly, especially now that I can do it while I'm awake." She glanced in Ares's direction before turning back to the goddess of love. "That is, when I'm not being hunted down and kidnapped."

Aphrodite smiled politely. "Your talent for swimming comes from my mother, Dione, who's quite impressed with you, by the way. She will be an advocate of yours for all time."

Therese frowned. "Have I met her?"

"She's the silver lady who stopped Ares from following you when you left Poseidon's palace with the bear," Than explained.

"Silver lady?" Therese shook her head. "I didn't see her. I was so focused on finishing the quest, I suppose."

"I think she arrived after you'd left," Ares said.

Therese glared at him. Than stifled a giggle. She was so cute when she was angry.

"And your courage comes from Ares," Aphrodite continued. "Like it or not, his blood runs through you, too."

Therese averted her eyes.

"Of course, your talent with the bow and arrow comes from Cupid." Aphrodite took a sip of her wine. "And another of your gifts is your love for others, which is quite profound, is it not, Ares?"

Ares nodded. "Yes. Quite profound, and a thorn in my side, I might add."

"But, darling, she gets that from me."

Than and Alecto exchanged amused smiles.

Ares stroked Aphrodite's long blond hair. "Yes, I know."

"And it's her most important quality," Aphrodite said defensively. "She couldn't fulfill her purpose as goddess of animal companions without it."

"Indeed," Ares said.

"A happy family reunion," Apollo interrupted. "But I'm afraid I've no time for it." He stood to go.

"Thank you for coming," Therese said, standing with the god of truth and shaking his hand. "Thank you so very much."

Apollo gave Than a silent prayer, "I don't believe you are rid of Ares."

Than prayed back as he stood and shook Apollo's hand, "Why?"

"Good bye, all." Apollo vanished.

Therese and Than remained standing.

Alecto joined them, "I, too, must get back to my work." The Fury vanished.

"Are you leaving so soon?" Aphrodite's question was directed at Therese.

"I have something I have to do," Therese replied. "A friend of mine needs help."

"Oh?" Aphrodite looked concerned.

"You remember Pete Holt? The one Cupid shot to make fall in love with me?" Therese turned a scowl in Ares's direction, and Than again stifled a smile at how cute she could be.

Aphrodite nodded.

"Well, I shot him with an arrow of hate, hoping to neutralize it, but he looked upon his sister first."

"That's terrible! Jen, the one whose father...?"

"Yes," Therese said. "So I transformed Pete into a dog and shot him with one of my companion arrows, which was great and all, but I thought I would be able to change him back, and I couldn't. So I'm going to find a way to do that."

"How?" Aphrodite asked.

"She's going on a secret quest," Than interrupted. The last thing they needed was for Hera to learn of Therese's plan before it was enacted. "And it's time sensitive. We need to go. Thanks again for meeting with us."

Than took Therese's hand and together they returned to his rooms. He sent a prayer of thanks to his sister before turning to Therese.

195

"You said too much," he told her.

"What do you mean? They wouldn't tell Hera, would they?"

He pushed her hair out of her eyes and gently kissed her cheek. "Probably not. But it's best to keep this adventure to ourselves." He decided not to share Apollo's warning with her. No need to make her any more anxious than she already was. "I'll get my sword and shield."

"And we should hop over to my room and grab my flute."

He kissed her again. "Sounds like a plan."

Chapter Thirty-Six: Atlas

After checking on Clifford and Jewels, Therese grabbed her flute case from beneath her bed, opened it, and assembled its three silver pieces.

"Ready?" Than asked.

"Outside the Marjorelle Garden, right?" she asked.

"Right."

Together they god traveled to Marrakesh, Morocco to pluck two apples from Hera's garden, but before the pines at the base of the Atlas Mountains came into view, an unexpected embrace pulled Therese away from her destination, and before she could blink, she was standing on a mountain peak on the tallest mountain for miles. More startling than her location was the proximity of the giant standing in front of her, looking down at her with a creepy smile and intense black eyes. The giant wore a white sarong at his hips, golden sandals, and nothing else but his curly black hair and beard. His arms were lifted up to the heavens, as though he were holding a bank of clouds. Then Therese realized who he was.

"Atlas?"

"Ah, you know my name," he said in a voice that was deep and loud enough to echo throughout the mountains. "Now tell me yours."

"Therese." She straightened her back and lifted her chin. "I'm the goddess of animal companions."

"Have you come to play your flute for me?"

She lifted her flute to study it, having forgotten it was in her hand. "No. I was actually on my way to play it for the Hesperides."

"My lovely daughters. How nice." He narrowed his intense black eyes. "But you must have another reason for visiting them. You must hope to pluck an apple."

Therese wasn't sure if she should admit this to the father of the Hesperides, so she said nothing, her throat suddenly tight.

"If you play for me on your flute, I'll get the apples for you," the Titan offered.

"Really?" She screwed her face up at him, not at all sure of his trustworthiness. She thought she recalled a story in which Atlas had tricked someone by making a similar offer.

"Yes. Can you imagine how boring it is to stand here day after day with no one to talk to, no music, no laughter? I receive very few visitors."

Therese thought it couldn't hurt to play a brief song, but she would then be on her way. She put the flute to her chin and blew across the hole, fingering a soft ballad she remembered from her sophomore year. Tears flooded the Titan's eyes and his creepy smile softened into a grateful one.

"That was beautiful," he said when she had finished.

"Thank you. And thanks for your offer, but I better be going now."

"Wait. Didn't you visit my daughters last summer and deceive them with that very flute?"

Therese's mouth fell open. She tried to god travel away, but her feet stayed glued to the ground. "Am I your prisoner?"

"Not his. Mine." Ares appeared beside her.

She dropped her flute and fitted an arrow to her bow, but Ares vanished before she could release it. He appeared again at her other side. She took aim again, but again, he vanished. He came up behind her, his hands pinning her arms to her side. She clutched her bow in one hand and the arrow in the other, but she could not lift her arms, nor could she god travel away.

"Why are you doing this?" she asked through gritted teeth. "You heard what the Fates said."

"As relieved as I am that you'll have no immortal children, I can't help but suspect it's because of what I'm about to do."

"Yeah? And what's that?"

He used his superior strength to force her to stand beside Atlas. Then he squeezed her wrists until she dropped her bow and arrow, and lifted her arms toward the bank of clouds.

"You'll be taking Atlas's place for a while." He nodded to the giant. "Ready?"

The Titan nodded back and slowly lowered the bank of clouds onto Therese's hands.

"No! Help! Than! Thanatos!" The clouds were heavier than they looked and she labored beneath them.

Atlas turned his intense eyes to her. "I'm sorry to leave you with this burden. Long ago, I was made to keep Uranus, the Sky, from mating with Gaia, the Earth. Now it's your turn."

"Wait! How do you know I won't drop Uranus and let him and Gaia have at it?" She lowered the clouds to her shoulders, her arms trembling from the weight.

Ares gave her a sardonic smile. "Because the first thing the Titans will do if they overpower the Olympians will be to destroy humankind, and you wouldn't want that on your back."

He and the Titan vanished, leaving her alone with the sky in her hands.

"No! Please! I have to help Pete! Please!" Why couldn't Than hear her cries, her prayers?

Chapter Thirty-Seven: The Garden

Than arrived outside of the Majorelle Garden in Marrakesh, Morocco where, unlike in Colorado where it was seven hours behind, the sun was rising above the Atlas Mountains. But where was Therese? They had just left her room in Colorado moments ago. He disintegrated to go back and look for her, but his other self went on, feeling for the entrance to the garden of the Hesperides, which was invisible to mortal eyes. The scent of pine was soon replaced with that of citrus, and the long rows of fruit trees came into view. With each step he took through the garden, Than disintegrated, so that by the time he saw the huge sprawling apple tree with its gnarly roots and branches, he was equal in number to Ladon's hundred heads.

The three daughters of Atlas awoke from where they lay curled between the roots, their beautiful figures so matched in color to the dark gray bark of the tree that they at first appeared to be nothing but gowns billowing in the breeze. Their eyes widened at the army Than had amassed, and they quickly sprang from the tree and disappeared.

Ladon, who had also been sleeping, opened his two hundred eyes and lifted his one hundred heads from where they'd been dripping from the branches like tree sap.

"I don't want to hurt you," Than warned, preferring a peaceful relinquishing of the apples to a slaughter. The beast was immortal and would return to his body in a few days, but if there were another way, he'd take it.

In case peace was not an option, he raised his one hundred swords. "I need two apples from the tree."

Ladon's heads struck in less time than it took to breathe, but Than spun out of reach and then brought his sword around. He managed to slice off a good third of the heads, but a moment's hesitation as he realized Therese was not at home in Colorado or at his rooms in the Underworld made him vulnerable. Ladon's fangs pierced through his trousers. Even though it was one bite, pain seared through all three hundred thousand of him everywhere he was in the world as the hot poison burned through his veins. He managed to slice off another third of the heads before his vision became blurry and he was struck again.

He multiplied himself into the billions, and like insects swarming its prey, he surrounded Ladon and the tree, crawling up the gnarly trunk to the highest branches. Though he could barely see, he climbed and swung, climbed and swung, an explosion of his disintegrated selves, all mercilessly attacking, long after, he soon realized, the dragon lay still.

He integrated into one at the garden, though he continued to carry out his duties for hundreds of thousands of souls. His vision was nearly gone, but he managed, so keen were his other senses and so familiar was his path through the Underworld. The Hesperides screamed from a distance as he looked with the last of his sight over the chopped bits of Ladon and at the blood dripping from the leaves and bark, and pooling on the grass near his feet. His vision became weaker and weaker as he escorted Ladon's soul to the Underworld. Than felt sorry for the beast, who was only doing his job, but he said nothing as he led him to Charon. The one Than at the garden amid the screams of the Hesperides quickly plucked two golden apples from the tree and returned to the safety of his chambers. Once the apples were well hidden, he asked Alecto to help him hunt for Therese.

Before he could set out on his journey, he found himself blind to the point that he could no longer find the souls calling to him.

In the next instant, he felt the transference of his duties as death to another, and he fell in a heap on his bed, feeling useless and afraid.

Chapter Thirty-Eight: The Goddess of Sleep

Therese struggled under the weight of the sky as the sun continued to climb over the Atlas Mountains, when suddenly the souls of the dying beckoned to her from all over the world, and she found herself disintegrating and dispatching to aid the dead. This could only mean one thing.

"Than!"

One of her dispatched to the garden of the Hesperides to look for him. Meanwhile, the one on the mountain summit multiplied into the twenties to better distribute the weight of the sky and ease her burden. Then she had the idea of stacking rocks to form pillars to take her place entirely. She disintegrated into thirty workers, each pulling out boulders from the sides of the mountain, cracking them by hitting them together to make flat edges, and stacking them up to equal her height. She built four columns along the peak of the mountain and then carefully lifted the sky from her shoulders and balanced the bank of clouds on the pillars of rock.

Back at Hera's garden, Therese was mortified by what she saw: Ladon chopped to bits, blood draping from the branches, and the three Hesperides weeping beneath the gnarly apple tree. The three nymphs looked up at her with their sad faces, their tears glinting in the morning sun, and before they could say a word, Therese took up her flute and played them a ballad to comfort them. Doing so wasted no time. She felt it was the least she could do. While she played, she disintegrated and dispatched to the Underworld.

As she neared the Underworld, she sensed Than in his bedroom and god traveled directly there. Relieved to find him all in one piece, she rushed to his side.

"Than? What's happened? Are you okay?" She leaned over where he lay on the bed, placed her hands gently on his chest, and looked into his face. That's when she noticed his eyes moving around in their sockets, apparently unable to focus on her. "You can't see!"

"Ladon's poison."

She brought her hand to her mouth to stifle a gasp. "How long will this last?"

"I don't know. Maybe forever. I need Apollo. But first, tell me. Where have you been? Are you alright?"

Therese shuddered. Forever? He could be blind forever? So in trying to save Pete, she'd ruined Than's life. She sank on the bed beside him resting her elbows on her knees, her face in her hands. "I can't believe this."

Than sat up on the edge of the bed beside her. "When I arrived in Morocco, you weren't there."

"Ares intercepted me and took me to Atlas. He forced me to take the Titan's place."

"What? Why? Are you still there now?"

"Yes, but I'm constructing pillars to hold the sky. I'm nearly done. Where can I find Apollo?"

"Damn that Ares! Damn him forever!" Than took a deep breath and blew it out. "First take the apple to Pete."

She jumped from the bed. "You got an apple?"

"Two. An extra to offer to Ares, like we planned." He told her where she could find them.

Therese took one and left the other hidden. "How can I give Pete the apple without killing him?"

"That's right. He'll die in your presence. Damn that Ares!" Then he turned his face up to the ceiling. "Hip we need you! It's urgent!"

"What can he do?" Therese asked, pacing.

"He can switch with you."

Hip appeared. "Why would I switch with her?"

Therese hadn't seen him in a while, and she'd forgotten how much he resembled his brother, even though they weren't identical: same height and build, same strong jaw and dark brows, and same sweet blue eyes, but where Than's hair was dark brown—nearly black—Hip's was golden.

"Please help us!" Therese said frantically. "Than's blind!"

"Blind?" Hip went to his brother's side and studied his face. "How?"

"Ladon's poison. Look, can you switch with Therese and be Death one more time so she can save her friend? I'll owe you another."

"Are we talking about Pete Holt?"

"How'd you know?" Therese asked.

"His sister, Jen. We've become quite close in her dreams. In fact, she's my favorite right now." He gave her his radiant smile and flirtatious wink.

"She's fragile, Hip," Therese said. "Please don't toy with her."

"Toy? I'm in love."

"Hip," Than interrupted. "We don't have time for this. Will you please just switch with her?"

"Will you get me a date with Jen?" he asked.

Therese rolled her eyes. "Are you serious? You want to break my friend's heart?"

"No. I want her to fall in love with me. Than, you, of all people, should understand. Why can't I find a partner, too?"

"You can't be serious," Than said. "You're not the type to settle down."

"People change."

"Look, whatever," Therese said with exasperation. "I'll get you the date. Now switch with me."

Hip took her hand and the transference of duty was immediate. Therese continued to disintegrate, but now, instead of guiding the souls of the dead, she was monitoring, and in some cases participating in, the dreams of hundreds of thousands of people all over the world. She disintegrated again and dispatched to the Holt place with the apple.

The Therese that remained behind stood before Hip with her mouth wide open. "This is so…surreal."

"Tell me about it," Hip said, laughing. "Now you know why I hate switching. Than definitely got the worse lot."

"You can leave now," Than said.

"Fine." Hip disappeared.

Therese turned to Than. "Tell me how I find Apollo. I can help Pete and look for Apollo at the same time."

"Hermes is best at finding gods in a hurry, and my father can summon Hermes in a flash."

Hades appeared near the stalagmite that held Than's clock and quill. "You called?" He took a closer look at Than. "Dear god, what happened to you?"

Than explained what happened in Hera's garden. In the next instant, Hermes arrived, followed by Persephone, who swooned over Than in a high-pitched, frantic voice.

"How can this be? How could this happen?"

"We need Apollo," Hades said. "The longer Ladon's poison runs through Thanatos's blood system, the worse are his chances for recovery."

"Yes, Lord Hades." Hermes disappeared.

205

Back at the Holt place, Therese hovered outside Jen's window to scope out the situation before entering. Jen and the golden retriever lay side by side in Jen's bed, sound asleep. Therese flew inside, picked up the dog, whose sleep was deepened by her presence, and god traveled to Pete's room. Then she entered Pete's dream, a bit frazzled to find him making out with Vicki's cousin Courtney in the hay in the barn with Stormy and Sassy looking on. It wasn't really Courtney, of course; it was a figment. Stormy and Sassy were also figments. Therese commanded them to show themselves. They transformed into three scaly eels, which swirled about the barn with hilarious laughter before flying away.

Pete sat up in the hay and looked at Therese, dumbfounded. "Therese?"

"Listen to me, Pete. I need you to eat this golden apple."

"But I'm not hungry." He stood up and wiped the hay from the back of his jeans. "I'd rather make out with you."

"But we're just friends, remember?"

"Can't we be friends with benefits?" He took her in his arms.

She held him back at arm's length, but gave him a smile. "So you're not in love with me anymore, right?"

"Love? Well, more like a little crush. Now are you gonna kiss me?"

"I'm with Than, remember?"

He frowned. "So that's a done deal? You sure? What do you know about him, anyway?"

"Quite a lot, actually. Now will you please try a bite of this apple?"

In the dream, she handed it to him, and he took a bite. In the awake world, Therese fed the apple to the sleeping dog. As soon as a single bite was swallowed, the golden retriever changed back into Pete Holt, the man.

"Oh, thank goodness," Therese whispered as she tucked Pete into bed. Tears flooded her eyes, and she batted them away with the back of her hands. She kissed Pete on the forehead. In the dream world, she hugged him, too, and told him she was sorry.

"Why are you sorry?" he asked.

"I just am." She pulled away. "Still friends?"

"Always." He winked.

Therese snapped her fingers and a figment obediently appeared in the form of Courtney. "I'm glad you two found each other."

"It's nothing serious," Pete said. "I've already told her I'm not ready for a relationship. Still too burned by you." He smiled, to let her know he would be alright.

More relief swept over Therese and, even in the dream world, her eyes filled with tears.

"See ya," she said, waving.

"See ya."

Therese decided to enter Jen's dream, too, to check on her. To her horror, she found a vicious cycle reeling round and round without end of Pete screaming hateful words to Jen, knocking over chairs. Then Pete's hands were at Jen's throat. Jen wriggled free, grabbed a gun, shot. Over and over, these same events occurred. Jen was stuck in the hellish cycle.

Therese intervened by appearing in the dream. First, she commanded the figment disguised as Pete to show itself and leave. Then she took the gun from Jen and told her everything was going to be okay.

Without transition, Jen was a little girl, maybe five or six, wearing a short simple dress and a pair of boots and milking a goat tied to the back of the house. Therese looked on from above, no longer in Jen's view. Mr. Holt, much younger and much handsomer, ambled from the barn.

"Where's your mama?" he asked her cheerfully.

"Store."

"And your brothers?"

"Out to pasture."

"Then why don't you come sit on Daddy's lap and let me tell you a story?"

Little Jen squealed with pleasure. She picked up the bucket of milk and skipped inside the house behind her father. Therese looked on, overcome with anxiety.

"Will you tickle me again?" Jen asked, pulling off her dress.

"I'll tickle you if you tickle me."

"Deal!"

Therese covered her mouth in horror as she watched the father molest the daughter in a way that made the daughter think it was fun, normal, and acceptable behavior. Five-year-old Jen enjoyed herself, laughing and smiling as though it were all a game. More tears fell from Therese's eyes as she realized now why Jen blamed herself. She'd been taught to enjoy her father's abuse and so felt responsible. Therese felt sorry for her friend, and helpless, too, until she had an idea.

"Figment, I command you to show yourself!" she said to the vision of Mr. Holt.

The eel-like creature whisked about the room, giggling before flying away.

Therese took on the form of Mr. Holt and approached Jen, whom Therese had transformed into her seventeen-year-old self wearing her favorite t-shirt and blue jeans. "Jen, I need to tell you something."

"Dad?"

"None of this was your fault. You were just a baby girl, and I was a messed up man, and I'm so sorry for hurting you."

Jen's face contorted into an expression of pain and misery. "I, I…"

"You don't have to say a thing, baby girl. You are a good girl. You've done nothing wrong. I'm entirely to blame. I can't apologize enough."

Therese could barely watch as Jen's body shook, her mouth open and gasping for air, her face white, then red, then white again. She cried and cried.

Therese went to pat her on the arm, but Jen cringed beneath the touch. That's when Therese decided to change back to her own form and comfort her friend.

"Therese?"

"It's going to be okay, Jen."

Jen threw her arms around Therese, and Therese held her for as long as it took.

At the same time Therese comforted Jen, she appeared before Carol, who had waited up on the couch in front of an old movie.

"I'm sorry I'm home so late." Even though Therese was in mortal form, her presence made it difficult for Carol to fight sleep.

"I'm..." yawn, "just...glad...you're...home." Carol's head fell back on the pillow tucked in the corner of the couch.

Therese pushed Carol's legs up in a comfortable position and rearranged the quilt over her. Then she turned off the television and went to check on her pets. Jewels's lamp had been turned off and Clifford's water bowl was still full. She stroked her sleeping pets and returned to the Underworld, where Apollo had arrived and was busy concocting a liquid remedy on an elaborate structure recently erected on Than's sideboard.

Apollo had already explained that he was using the venom from Python—a snake he defeated centuries ago and whose venom he preserved and has often used—to create an antidote that should work on Ladon's poison, since the two serpent dragons shared the same mother. Steam boiled up from a purple liquid bubbling in a glass beaker. Apollo took a glass syringe the size of a turkey baster and siphoned some of the purple liquid into a test tube, which he then added in gradations to another beaker filled with dark red syrup. When the syrup turned orange, he handed the beaker to Than and told him to drink all of it.

Therese was momentarily startled from the scene in the Underworld by her aunt's dream, which unexpectedly pulled her in. A big winding staircase made of solid oak floated from the floor of what appeared to be her home in Colorado, except each room was decorated slightly differently, and there were extra rooms, too, which Therese had never seen before. She knew the man and woman on either side of her aunt were figments, but they looked so much like her mom and dad that she hung in midair at the base of the hovering stairs and watched, dumbstruck, as they ascended with Carol to the next level.

Therese crept up the stairs and looked around. On every level, there were toddlers sitting on the wooden floors playing with toys and laughing. One grabbed a rope and swung through the air, over the staircase, and landed in a net, like the ones used at the circus for the trapeze artists and tight-rope performers. Then she saw Richard in the kitchen downstairs at the kitchen sink, his hands covered in raw meat and seasonings.

"Where's the olive oil?" he asked.

"Second cabinet to the right of the sink!" Carol called from above.

Therese caught up to her aunt and the figments and watched silently from behind.

"This is the conservatory," Carol was saying. "And over here is the library."

"You've added quite a few books to our collection," her father, or rather the figment, said.

210

"Here's the gymnasium," Carol said. "And across from it is the indoor pool where Therese practices her strokes."

"Does she miss us?" her mother asked.

Therese stopped dead in her tracks, which somehow attracted Carol's attention.

Carol turned to her. "Therese?"

"I do miss you, Mom," Therese whispered, her voice caught in her throat. "I miss you, too, Dad."

"I'm just showing them around," Carol said. "The nursery for Lynn is right this way."

Babies and toddlers swung by on the rope and bounced up in the air from the net below. Richard called up to locate other spices and household items, and Carol continued to point out one extravagant room after another—a game room, a sitting room, a sewing and craft room, a sculpture room—but Therese could only stare at the backs of the figments beside her, feeling the old familiar longing for her parents.

"Therese?" Than said, taking her face in his hands. "Are you okay?"

Persephone stood beside her son with an arm draped over his shoulders.

"Can you see?" Therese asked, pulling her thoughts away from the dream.

"Yes! Well, it's still a bit blurry."

"It may take a few days for your vision to return to normal," Apollo explained.

Therese turned to the god of light and gave him a beaming smile. "Thank you! I can't thank you enough!"

"Perhaps some time when things settle down around here, you can play your flute with me while I play my lyre."

"I'd like that very much," Therese said.

"So would I," Hades said. "We haven't had music down here in many years. I look forward to having a musician living among us."

Therese felt her cheeks get hot. She couldn't wait to be with Than, but her aunt's dream pulled her away again.

"Mom and Dad?" They turned briefly to look down at her from the steps of the staircase and to give her smiles, and then they continued toward the top with Carol.

"And this is the puzzle room, where we like to have tea..."

Hip appeared and took Therese's hand. The dream vanished, and she was immediately integrated into one. She was no longer the goddess of sleep. And she was no longer the goddess of death. Hip and Than had resumed their respective offices.

Chapter Thirty-Nine: Halloween Night

Therese stayed with Than for a few more hours and then returned home where she slept for the first time since becoming a goddess. She tried to manipulate her dreams, searching for her mom and dad, but nothing went right, and she woke to the sun streaming through her windows.

Maybe she would visit them in the Underworld. The idea had occurred to her before, but she'd been afraid. She knew they wouldn't recognize her, and she was afraid she wouldn't be able to handle the blank look in their eyes. Even now, she wasn't sure she could do it.

Over the next few weeks, while Hermes attempted to secure a safe and secret meeting for her with Ares, Therese took more tests online and groomed Stormy, pleased to find the Holts relatively back to normal. Therese also practiced driving with her uncle Richard. In fact, she fell into a comfortable routine: morning walks with Clifford, breakfast with Carol and Richard, and grooming Stormy and visits with the Holts until noon. Then it was lunch back home with Carol, online tests and papers in the afternoon, and driving with Richard until dinner. She spent dinner and evenings with Carol and Richard, and then nights in her room with Than. Since god travel made her vulnerable, Than preferred to come to her room rather than she to his just in case Ares had something else up his sleeve.

Throughout the day, Therese also continued to answer the prayers related to animal companions and to inspire people and animals as often as she could. She looked forward to a day when she could freely god travel so she could use her bow and arrow to help people and animals more fully love one another.

Carol's most recent doctor's appointment showed promising test results and healthy progress for the baby, which, though not wholly unexpected by Therese was nevertheless a surprise. The mood around the house was positive and hopeful, and Carol's doctor even allowed her to get off bed rest. With her due date in early November—a few short weeks away—she kept herself busy shopping for the baby.

Hermes chose Halloween night for the meeting, because the other gods would be distracted by the festivities. According to Hermes, just about every god and goddess, from the most powerful Olympian to the smallest nymph, liked to dress up in costume and roam the cities in playful camaraderie with humans.

While it was still nighttime on Therese's side of the world, the people on the eastern half of the globe were already well into the first day of November, so Hermes chose The Philippine Islands for the meeting place—specifically, Boracay, on a dinner boat not far from the island.

Hermes joined Than and Therese at a round table covered in a white linen cloth and set for four. A bottle of wine had been brought and poured in glasses for all three by a beautiful sea nymph already familiar with Hermes. The nymph had radiant caramel skin, long black hair, and black eyes framed with lush lashes.

Therese took a sip of wine and waited, clutching Hera's apple in a blue velvet pouch in her lap. Ares was late.

Than squeezed her free hand on his thigh beneath the table. He was trying to reassure her, but she could tell he was nervous, too. She gave him a smile. He smiled back. Hermes cleared his throat and tried to make small talk.

"The fishing off this island is supposed to be the best in the world."

"I don't doubt it," Than said.

"Maybe you and I should go sometime," Hermes said.

"Why, cousin!" Than said with surprise. "You've never invited me before. What's changed?"

214

Hermes frowned and took a sip of wine. "You always kept to yourself. Therese has brought you out, so to speak."

Than nodded and cleared his throat, unable to deny the truth in what his cousin said. He had kept to himself, but he had done so partly because he did not feel accepted by the other gods. He supposed he should have tried harder to help them get to know him, to show them that he wasn't as gloomy as his office.

Than distracted himself from the anxiety he felt by gazing at Therese. She looked beautiful in her white sundress beneath the afternoon sun, her green eyes sparkling from the gleam off the sea. The gentle breeze lifted her hair around her face like bronze flames. He couldn't resist reaching out and touching it. She met his eyes and gave him her nervous smile. He wished their meeting with Ares was behind them, and then they could enjoy the breathtaking scenery, the delicious food about to be served, the wine, and each other.

As the salad plates heaped with cold greens and tomatoes were brought out, Ares appeared in the empty seat at their table. The nymph, used to such things, did not flinch.

"I was beginning to think you wouldn't show," Hermes complained.

"You said you'd make it worth my while," Ares replied. "I find that hard to believe, unless your plan is to betray these two and turn the girl over to me."

"I'm not a girl," Therese said with narrowed eyes. "I'm a god, and I won't have you talk about me like I'm not here."

Than's throat tightened. He was proud of her, but he was also afraid. He squeezed her hand in his lap. She squeezed back.

Ares ignored Therese's remark and took a bite of the salad. "Delicious. Good choice, Hermes. I like this boat, this view of the island, and its beach. I see beautiful women not far away. The pristine sky

215

stretches for miles. Maybe I'll bring Aphrodite here some time. I think she's grown tired of Paris."

The others ate their salads, too. They were anxious to get the meeting over with, but were afraid to begin.

Plates of grilled fish smothered in white sauce and rice were brought out next. Therese found it difficult to enjoy her food. As good as it tasted, her stomach was churning with fear and dread. Would Ares accept the apple? Could they finally call a truce and live their lives in peace?

Hermes and Ares spoke of water sports and volcanos and other topics which seemed to put Ares in a good mood. Therese began to relax a little too. She managed to finish most of her plate just as the dessert was brought out.

She took another sip of wine, feeling as though she would not be able to eat another bite. She watched Ares scoop the chocolate covered strawberries and cream into his mouth. He occasionally ran a hand through his red hair. She realized then that his hair and hers were the same shade. She wondered if his blood ran through her from her father or mother. She had never thought to ask.

As he finished his dessert, she could wait no more. "We've asked you here to offer a truce."

"And how do you propose to leverage it?" Ares dabbed his chin and lips with his white linen napkin.

Therese took her hand from Than's grasp and opened the blue velvet pouch to reveal Hera's golden apple of immortality.

Ares's mouth dropped open. "I thought the mission was a failure."

"And now you see you were wrong," she replied.

Ares looked first at Hermes, then at Than, and back again to Therese. "Is it authentic?"

"Absolutely," Than said. "Do you need us to bring in Apollo?"

"No. I can tell with my own eyes. I just find it hard to believe you managed to get this apple without Hera's knowledge."

"I'm sure she knows," Than said. "I have felt her watching me ever since I took it."

"And if I take it from you, I will incur her wrath."

"She did nothing to Artemis," Hermes said. "What could she do to you that she couldn't to Artemis?"

"As her son, I often make alliances with her. Artemis has never cared for Hera."

Therese and Than exchanged worried glances.

Than asked, "Do you reject our offer?"

Ares seemed to consider it for a moment. Therese returned her hand to Than's and gripped it tightly.

The boat pitched to one side, knocking over the glasses on the table, except for the one belonging to Ares, as he held it in his hand. Red wine soaked into the white table cloth. Ares wore a smile on his face where the others looked confused. Across the horizon, Zeus's chariot led by four horses dropped from the sky and glided across the waves toward their boat. The four black stallions stampeded from the sky, their manes lifting in the wind behind them like dark flames. The air filled with the sound of a loud train. As the chariot neared, Therese saw Hera held the reins in one hand and a whip in the other. Her golden crown sat firmly on her head, her red hair fastened in a bun. A gold silk gown billowed at the sleeves against the wind. She was coming for her apple.

Therese knew that if Hera took her apple back, Therese would have nothing left to bargain for her safety. She glanced at Hermes and Than, wondering how the three of them would fare against Queen Hera and the god of war. She took a second glance at Hermes, unsure if she could count on his support, since he often favored neutral ground.

Wishing she had her sword and shield, she sent a distress prayer to Hephaestus. To her surprise, the god of the forge appeared in person, bearing not only her weapons, but Than's and his own. Then Athena appeared beside Than, her sword drawn at the ready. Ares's smile faded.

Although Therese firmly held the apple, it left her hand and appeared across the table on Ares's empty dessert plate. Before she or Than could retrieve it, Ares took it up. The boat leveled as Hera approached. Then a massive wave arose from the sea, and a silver hand snatched the apple from Ares's fist. The apple floated on the wave in the silver hand twenty feet above them before Dione showed herself, emerging from the wave as a giant silver gleam. In another moment, a second chariot appeared on the opposite horizon, and by the time Dione's wave settled itself back into the sea like a soft blanket and she returned to her original size, Poseidon drew his chariot beside her and brandished his sword, pointing it directly at Ares.

"So much for our secret meeting," Hermes muttered.

"Give me back my apple!" Hera commanded from her chariot, which was alongside the boat.

"I will keep it with me, thank you," Dione said in her sing-song voice. "It deserves to rest beside Hippolyta's golden girdle in the bottom of the sea, safeguarded from all who would use it unwisely."

Therese glanced anxiously at Than. If Dione kept the apple, how would Therese protect herself from Ares?

As if the silver lady read her mind, Dione said, "Ares, I know you wish for balance among the gods as well as the people of the world so that one power will not dominate over another but will always be in conflict. I swear on the River Styx to keep this apple in neutral territory until it is needed to restore balance."

Ares stood up, and pointed at Therese. "Her very presence among us unsettled the balance."

"That's where you're wrong," Than said, also standing.

All eyes turned to him.

"You witnessed Therese face off against her parents' murderer two summers ago. We all did. If she carried vengeance in her heart, we would have seen it then. You have nothing to fear by her presence."

Ares scrutinized Therese and then Than. He opened his mouth to speak, and then didn't.

Hephaestus put a hand on Than's shoulder. "The boy speaks the truth."

"You need to let it go, Ares," Athena said. "There's nothing more to fight about."

"I don't want vengeance!" Therese said. "I just want to be happy with Than. I swear!"

"You're an oath breaker," Ares said, scowling.

"She broke no oath," Athena said. "You have nothing to fear from her."

"Fear?" Ares scoffed. "She's just a girl. I don't fear her."

"Then we're done here," Than said.

"I want my apple!" Hera screamed.

Ares rolled his eyes. "Shut up, Mother!"

Before Hera could object, Ares climbed into her chariot and took the reins, leading them back into the sky across the horizon.

Therese turned to Than and the others, and they exchanged the smiles of victors.

Chapter Forty: Goddess at Large

Therese hovered above a dilapidated townhouse on a pock-marked street corner in Sant A'gata Bolognese, Italy with an arrow fitted to her bow. The tabby cat named Belle, from the Lamborghini Museum, sat on the front stoop lapping up milk the boy Luis had given her while his mother was away. Therese spotted the woman with her meager groceries walking on the sidewalk among the other people. The woman stopped at a corner to wait for the traffic to clear, and then continued on her way. As soon as she reached the front of her house and spotted the tabby, Therese let the arrow fly. It pierced the woman's heart.

"Well, hello, kitty," the woman said cheerfully to Belle in her native tongue. "Are you cold out here? Come inside and I'll make a fire."

Luis opened the door with his mouth agape, having heard his mother's voice. He watched in silent bewilderment as the tabby followed his mother inside the house.

Therese later found the boxer whose owner beat him. The man returned home from work one day in his tiny sports car, and as he parked in his garage and carried his briefcase indoors, Therese hovered, invisible, in the kitchen above the dog, who lay forlornly with his head on his paws near an empty bowl. When his human entered the house, his tail, which had once wagged excitedly at this time of day, tucked under him as he shivered and whined. Therese took aim and shot the man before he had opened his mouth to complain about the noise, and what came out was a surprise to the dog.

"Are you hungry, Butch? Come here and let me have a hug."

Tears sprang to Therese's eyes as she watched the boxer lift his head and dare to approach his human. When the man wrapped his arms around the dog, the tail, for the first time in months, began to wag.

Zeus had denied Therese the power of disintegration, apparently still troubled by Than's reaction to the Cyclopes and worried another office with such power might prove a threat. But he did revoke his decision to banish the two of them from Mount Olympus, though Than's annual punishment at the hands of the maenads would stand.

Ten days after the confrontation with Ares on the dinner boat off Boracay, Lynn was born at eight pounds, four ounces, twenty inches long, with wisps of red hair and blue-green eyes. She was healthy in every way, and the joy in Therese's Colorado home carried the other three members through the adjustments necessary to accommodate a new little addition to the household. Therese helped with nighttime feedings, since she rarely slept, and after she obtained her driver's license, was able to run errands into Durango for more diapers and formula. Soon, she was doing most of the grocery shopping for the family, which she didn't mind, since it took her very little time to locate the items on Carol's list. She also found she enjoyed driving the red Honda Civic Carol and Richard had bought her a year ago, and she would often take Jen, and sometimes even Bobby, into town with her.

Though Therese was also busy finishing her coursework, grooming Stormy, and working at her new job at the animal rescue shelter, the freedom to god travel made it easy for her to respond to prayers from both humans and animals all over the world. And she always found special time every day of the week to be with Than.

In April, when Lynn was nearly six months old, Therese's seventeenth birthday arrived, and Than surprised her by getting Hip to take his place so Than could attend her party with her family. Carol and Richard hadn't seen Than since the summer before last, and it filled Therese with happiness to have him there, her family complete. The Holts also came—all except Mr. Holt, of course, who now lived permanently at the assisted living center—and Ray and Todd and a few other friends from Therese's swim team.

After Richard's grilled burgers and Carol's homemade fries were served and eaten and the Happy Birthday song sung and the cake cut, and while the guests sat around a fire pit on the deck beneath the countless stars, finishing off their cake and ice cream, Than asked if he could have everyone's attention. Even Baby Lynn was silent.

He stood in the middle of the group near the fire pit with Therese beside him. "All of you already know what a special person Therese is. She'd do anything for her friends and family and pets. She also helps others when she can. Her compassion seems boundless. Most of you also know I fell in love with Therese two summers ago when I visited the Melner Cabin next door and took a job as a horse handler for the Holts. Therese and I have grown close in the nearly two years we've known each other." He looked at her and smiled.

She smiled back, a bit nervous, wondering what all this speech-making was about and beginning to suspect the reason.

When he went down on one knee and pulled out a tiny black box from his trouser pocket, her heart stopped.

He opened the box to reveal a beautiful tear-drop diamond ring on a delicate gold band. "Therese, I love you with all my heart. I knew the moment we met that you were the one. Will you marry me?"

Her family and friends remained silent for a moment as she gazed back at Than with her mouth open, speechless. Finally, some of her friends whooped and hollered and someone said, "Answer him!"

Therese went down on her knee beside him, took his hand in hers, and said, "It would be impossible for someone to love another more than I love you. I want to spend eternity with you."

Everyone around them applauded. Someone whistled—Jen, Therese realized. Therese's aunt and uncle appeared happy but concerned. Than took Therese by the arm and helped her to her feet.

"Just so you don't freak, Carol and Richard, I promise to wait another year. This time next year, when I turn eighteen, we'll be married, and all of you are invited."

Than gave her a quizzical look, but she kissed him before he could say anything.

Later that night, when they were alone in her room after he had received his office back from Hip, Than wanted to know why she wanted to wait a year.

"A year to us is nothing," she said, sitting beside him on her bed. "And it will mean so much to them. Eighteen is considered the age when a person becomes an adult. I should be done with my coursework this summer, so I can graduate, and I can spend time with Lynn before I move out. They need me right now."

"But what about our plans to travel the world together?"

"We can do that while I'm planning our wedding. Believe me, my aunt and uncle are going to expect a traditional wedding. Do you suppose the Olympians will come?"

"They'd be too curious to miss."

"So you're okay with waiting?" she asked. "Because if it bothers you, I'll marry you now. I don't want to disappoint you, Than."

"You could never disappoint me." He kissed her gently on the lips. "Besides, we said we'd wait till you graduated high school, and your eighteenth birthday is really only another six months from your estimated graduation date. And, as you said, you should spend Lynn's first year here at home, bonding with her. She's your sister, after all."

Therese circled her arms around Than's neck and pressed her lips hard against his. "I love you so much! Sometimes it hurts and feels good all at the same time!"

"I know exactly what you mean." He kissed her back, and in between kisses he said, "That's how I felt when the maenads ripped me apart. It hurt like hell, but knowing it meant being with you forever made it feel good, too."

Therese found herself spending more and more time in the Underworld, preparing Than's rooms for her official move in date. The two rats that perched on her shoulders during her final challenge last summer found her again, and they sometimes flew with her on her missions to help humans and animals to better love one another. This gave her the idea of inviting along Clifford, who at first found flight and god travel disconcerting, but who eventually adjusted and even came to enjoy their missions together. A few weeks before the wedding, Therese shot an arrow into Jewels and gave her the gift of immortality. Therese set up her tank in their chambers in the Underworld to help her adjust to her new quarters. She'd been gradually moving more and more of her things from Colorado into her new rooms, and on occasion solicited Charon's assistance with some of her bulkier items. Luckily, Cerberus took an immediate liking to Clifford, and the two of them sometimes played together outside of the gates while Therese organized and decorated her rooms. Than surprised her by bringing in the souls of plants he'd been collecting and by giving her the idea of bringing Stormy.

"What?" Mrs. Holt asked Therese where they stood in the barn by Stormy's stall. It was late March, two short months before the wedding.

"I want to take Stormy to Texas," she said. "I promise to take excellent care of him."

Mrs. Holt looked from Pete to Jen to Bobby and back again to Therese. "Well, I must say I never expected this. When we gave him to you, I thought he'd stay here with us."

"But we did give him to her," Pete said. "Didn't we? Or did you do it in name only."

Mrs. Holt shook her head. "No. Stormy belongs to Therese, and if she wants to take him to Texas, she can."

"He's almost two, after all," Jen said. "Old enough to leave Sassy."

Therese couldn't explain that she planned to visit Sassy often, via god travel. She also had to lie and say Than would drive up to Texas with a trailer to transport Stormy, when in reality, she'd shoot him with an arrow before taking him directly to the Underworld. Although most mortal horses weren't strong enough to ride until they were four, as an immortal being, Stormy could handle Therese, especially since most of the time they'd be in the air.

Before the night that she took Stormy, Therese switched duties with Hip once more so he could go as a mortal to the upper world and take Jen on a date. Jen was pleased to meet Than's twin brother. Therese could tell Jen recognized him from her dreams.

"I saw him coming," Jen told Therese one spring afternoon as they kayaked together on the Lemon reservoir. "I've been dreaming about Hip for months."

"Long distance relationships can be difficult," Therese warned, afraid for her friend. If Hip broke Therese's heart, she'd punch him, and now that she was a god, she knew it would hurt.

"Well, it was just one date," Jen said. "But you never know, do you?"

One day while she was moving more things into the Underworld, her rats jumped from her shoulders and ran along the Phlegethon through winding chambers toward the Lethe. They didn't beckon Therese, like they sometimes did, to show her something new down there she hadn't seen before, but, she followed them anyway, curious. Long before the rats joined their friends in some dark crevice, Therese noticed the Fields of Elysium and the multitudes of souls sharing their common illusions. With her keen goddess eyesight, she spotted the souls of her parents picnicking beneath a tree. Her father scribbled notes inside a book, and her mother pinched a flower between her fingers, breaking off petals. Therese knew they would not recognize her, but she decided it was time to say goodbye. Without touching the Lethe streams, lest she lose her memory as well, Therese flew to their tree and said hello.

"Hello," her mother said.

"Would you like to hear a poem?" her father asked.

Therese smiled. "Yes."

Her father read from where he had written in his book:

A constellation of three

Hung in the sky

Sparkling happily

Ever nigh.

Their light shone

For years and years

Long after time

Had taken the spheres.

Look in the sky

And see all three

Sparkling happily.

Her father looked up from his book. "What do you think?"

Tears flooded her eyes and rolled down her cheeks. "It's beautiful."

"I think you made her cry," her mother said to her father.

Therese batted the tears with the back of her hands. "That's okay. It was lovely. And these are happy tears."

Her father returned to his scribbling and her mother to breaking apart her flower. Therese whispered goodbye and floated away.

Two weeks before the wedding, Therese had completely moved everything she was taking with her to her chambers in the Underworld. She flew through the air on Stormy's back with her rats on her shoulders, Clifford in the saddle in front of her, and her quiver and bow over her shoulder. She looked down at her aunt and uncle preparing for dinner with Lynn scooting around in her walker cooing "Terry!" her name for Therese. Then she turned and looked through the earth and into the Underworld, where Than lit candles at their golden table, opened a bottle of wine, and turned on the CD player Therese had given him as a present. Jewels listened from her tank. Therese couldn't be happier about the family she was leaving (though she would often visit) and the one she would soon be making with the love of her life. She sailed through the air as the sun set in the west and rose in the east, both which she could see at once.

THE END

Please enjoy the first chapter of the next book in the series, *The Gatekeeper's House*:

THE GATEKEEPER'S HOUSE
Chapter One: Under Attack

Therese stood in the doorway, twirling a strand of her red hair round and round her index finger. There was only one bed in the center of Hecate's room. That could be a problem, even though Therese only slept about once a week.

"Maybe this wasn't such a good idea." Therese took a step back, knocking her quiver and bow against the cold stone wall.

"It will be fine." Hecate skipped forward and snatched up Therese's bag. "You can unpack your things in my closet." When she spun around toward the back of the room, her black and white hair fanned out around her slim shoulders.

Hecate didn't look like a witch or a hag or the dozens of other descriptions Therese had found on Google while visiting her family and friends in Colorado a month ago. She was an inch taller than Therese, and, in spite of the white streaks in her hair, she looked young, closer to Hermes's age, mid-twenties, with a delicate nose and thin lips. Therese knew Hecate was ancient—older than Than—but one thing she'd learned since becoming the goddess of animal companions was that immortal beings aged at different rates from humans and from one another.

"You aren't what I was expecting," Therese said with a smile.

"Mortals get me confused with Than's sister, Melinoe. That's probably it. Were you expecting someone more terrifying?"

Therese pulled her eyebrows together in confusion. "Do you mean Megaera?"

Hecate's face broke into a grin. "Those two are nothing alike." Then, in a somber voice, Hecate added, "I'm not surprised Than never mentioned Melinoe."

"Well that makes one of us," Therese said. How could he omit such an important detail? She'd told Than everything about herself and her family. Why wouldn't he have ever mentioned Melinoe? "Does she live down here, too?"

"She used to, until Hades banished her a few centuries ago. Now she lives on the outskirts of the Underworld in a cave on Cape Matapan."

"And that is…"

"On the southernmost tip of Greece." Hecate stepped forward. "Where are my manners? Meg will scold me later. Please come on inside. It's so nice to have company. I get lonely here when Persie moves in with Hades." Hecate slipped Therese's bag behind a wooden door, as though she wished to give Therese no opportunity to change her mind. "In the springs and summers on Mount Olympus, Persie and I share rooms with Demeter. Down here, I have a lot of time to myself."

Therese looked around the chamber for the first time, its dome ceiling high and covered with dancing shadows, cast by the light of the Phlegethon, the river of fire. A stream ran from an upper crevice down a series of rocks and pooled in a six-foot-wide basin before thinning and disappearing behind another smooth boulder.

"That's where I wash," Hecate explained. "The spring is fresh and good enough to drink."

Beside the basin and curled on a pillow was a small animal, a cute brown fur ball Therese had never seen. "Who's this?"

"Galin, my polecat. This is the time when she likes to sleep."

"I won't disturb her, then."

"My dog is awake and around here somewhere." Hecate glanced about the room. "Cubie? Where are you?"

A black Doberman pinscher with tall ears and a long tail crawled out from beneath the one big bed.

"There she is." Hecate reached over and patted the dog on the head. "Were you spying on us?"

"Absolutely," the dog answered.

Hecate laughed. "Cubie, this is Therese."

"Pleasure," the dog said.

"Likewise." Therese stroked Cubie's back, wishing Clifford had taken her seriously when she'd announced that she was moving out of Than's rooms. Instead, he'd given her an unconcerned stare as she had said *goodbye* and *I mean it this time*. "I have a dog, too. Maybe you would like to meet him."

"Is he intelligent?" Cubie asked.

"He's pretty smart." As the goddess of animal companions, Therese had met quite a lot of dogs, and she felt positive that Clifford was as smart as any of them.

"But probably not as smart as Cubie," Hecate said. "She was once the Queen of Troy."

Before Therese could ask why a former Queen of Troy was now a dog, the floor trembled beneath their feet, followed by a loud *boom*.

Therese clutched the wall as Hecate fell back on the bed and shouted, "Ahhh!"

"What was that?" Therese asked when the floor stabilized.

"I don't know." Hecate's voice was frantic. "I can't get a prayer through to Hades or to Persie."

Therese tried, too, but sensed no response. Blood pounded in her head as the ground began to quake again. She clutched the locket at her throat and prayed to Athena, but got no answer.

"Will these walls hold?" She glanced up at the ceiling, a host of scenarios playing through her mind. If the walls of the Underworld were to crumble, what would happen to its billions of inhabitants, including the souls of her mom and dad?

230

"Where are they—Hades and Persephone?" Therese asked.

Hecate winced as another *boom* sounded throughout the chamber. "Mount Olympus."

Just then, a crack ran across the ground, up the wall, and through the dome ceiling.

"It's going to collapse!" Therese shouted.

Small chunks of the ceiling fell on the bed, on the golden table by the hearth, and in the water basin, causing Galin to leap from her pillow and into Hecate's arms.

"Clifford and Jewels!" Therese cried. "They're in Than's rooms." Her stomach balled into a knot when she imagined them harmed.

"I'll go with you." Hecate set Galin down on the bed and spoke to the shivering weasel. "You and Cubie go to Demeter's winter cabin, and wait for me there. Okay?"

More rocks crumbled down the walls as a series of *booms* sounded throughout the chamber. The stream, which once ran gently down the wall, shot out, spraying in all directions.

"I'm not leaving you!" Galin returned to her mistress's arms.

"Nor I!" Cubie declared.

Soaked and trembling, the four of them rushed down the winding path along the Phlegethon, dodging the falling rocks. Cracks chased them all across the walls, and loud *booms* shuddered through the air. Therese was afraid to pray to Than, worried he'd god travel straight into danger. Even in her limited experience, she knew that if you arrived at a point occupied by solid mass, such as a large boulder, your body composition would momentarily meld with it. She'd discovered this problem when she once arrived in a brick wall. It had taken over an hour to recover, and the pain had been excruciating.

She found Clifford barking nervously by the hearth. "Come on, boy! We've got to get Stormy!"

Therese carried Jewels like a football in the crook of one arm as the group scurried down the narrow passageways toward the stables. She wondered if Than would be angry with her for not calling to him right away. He was already angry with her, and she didn't want to put another rift between them.

As they passed by the intersection of the Lethe and the Styx, deities cried out, and, although Therese and Hecate slowed down and searched the waters, they could not find the source of the cries. Cubie said she'd stay behind and keep searching.

When Therese rounded a corner, a colony of bats whirred up from a crevice below and fluttered past them, and then out climbed Tizzie, up from Tartarus with blood dripping down one arm.

"What is happening?" Tizzie demanded, her black serpentine curls covered in dust.

"We don't know," Therese replied.

"Well that's just great," Tizzie said, waving her hands. "The souls are in chaos. And if the pit ruptures, the Titans will be unleashed. Where the devil is my father?"

"Mount Olympus," Hecate said, dodging a falling rock that landed with a clack beside her.

Sensing Stormy's danger, Therese sent a prayer to Tizzie as she hustled toward the stables, explaining why she was on the run instead of god traveling to the gate.

I'll meet you at Cerberus, Therese added.

The three judges floated by her in their long robes headed in the opposite direction, toward the gate. Perhaps their demigod status kept them from god travel, she thought. Hecate was no longer behind her as Therese reached the stables with Clifford and Jewels. When she opened the wooden door, she found the walls had completely collapsed, and

Stormy lay on his side crushed beneath the rubble with blood pouring from his flanks.

***

Among the weeping women and children, Than pulled the soul of the Chinese man from the limp body on the bed. As sorry as he felt for those left behind, Than's own troubles distracted him beyond measure. He tried to put the doubts out of his mind, but with no success. They appeared, against his will: *Therese had used him so she could become a god. She had never loved him as he loved her. The death of her parents, and so many after, had motivated her to find a way around her own mortality.*

He ushered the soul across the heavens and then down through the deep chasm, where hundreds of his disintegrated selves led other souls from different parts of the world. Like a great machine—the greatest conveyor belt imaginable—he swept along, an automatic cog in the wheel of life. And there below him on his raft, long pole in hand, was his fellow cog, Charon, ready to carry the souls to their judgment.

For centuries, he'd done this same work, longing for a change, and now that he'd finally found his wish, he was only more miserable.

Therese never meant to marry him. He'd been a fool.

In the weeks since she moved in, her eighteenth birthday and their wedding date had come and gone. Therese had said she wasn't ready, postponing their marriage indefinitely. When he asked her why, she had repeated, "I'm not ready."

Than was a patient god. Although disappointed, he could wait for as many years as Therese needed. But it wasn't her *spoken* objection that had his stomach in knots and his emotions unstable; it was the physical distance she put between them of late that made him shiver and regret the day he'd met her.

How could the same touch of his hands on her that had once made her smile and cling to him cause her to avert her eyes and pull away? If she once loved him, it was clear she did no longer.

Aphrodite had warned him this might happen.

As he neared Charon, he noticed Cerberus whining, and beside him stood his sister Tizzie. Then he saw a great explosion beyond the gates, and red and orange sparks flew through the sky. Rocks tumbled down the walls of the chasm, like the beginning of an avalanche. In all the centuries Than had lived in the Underworld, he'd never witnessed anything like this before.

"Charon," Than said. "What's happening?"

"I believe the Underworld is under attack," the old man replied in his husky, gravelly voice.

At that moment, Than sensed Stormy's death in the stables, and he disintegrated and dispatched where he found Therese, with Jewels clutched to her chest and Clifford barking hysterically at the crushed body that belonged to Stormy.

"What in the hell is going on?" Than asked.

"I don't know! We can't reach your parents. We've got to get out of here."

Before Than could respond, a thick black boulder loosened from the ceiling and landed squarely on Therese's head, knocking her and the tortoise to the floor. The tortoise slid across the ground, spinning on its back, and stopped several feet away, safe from harm, but Than heard the crunch and thud of Therese's body beneath the weight of the massive rock. His heart stopped beating as he held his breath and stared in shock.

"Father!" he shouted into the falling debris surrounding him. He felt like a helpless, desperate child. "Father!"

***

234

Hypnos lifted the saddle onto the beast and tightened the tack. He still wasn't used to the sharp smell of hay and feces, stirred about by the brushing by humans of the other beasts surrounding him. It wasn't a bad smell, really. Having spent most of his life in the Dreamworld, where sensory perceptions were dulled by a degree of separation between the mind and the body, he rather liked the pungent assault on all of his senses, not just the olfactory ones. Besides, his eyes were continually pleased by the prettiest girl he'd ever seen who was now bent over in front of him. The corners of his mouth twitched, and he fought the urge to slap her on the rump. Instead, he patted Hershey, the horse in his charge, and told him what a good boy he was, as he'd often heard the other humans say to their beasts.

Hip was grateful to the old Holt woman for taking him on as a horse handler yesterday when he'd shown up, unannounced. He'd finally won his father's permission to follow in Than's footsteps to journey to the Upperworld as a mortal in a pursuit of a queen. Whether Hip would actually marry her was a different story. Hip realized that his brother had the right idea in finding a way to spend time in the Upperworld, and Hip wanted his turn. All these years of visiting girls in the Dreamworld didn't compare to the feeling of being in the physical presence of one.

Centuries ago, he'd come close to marrying one of Aphrodite's youngest Graces, Pasithea, but she overwhelmed him with her neediness, and he finally broke off their relationship. Since then, he'd been content playing with mortals in their dreams, but his brother's recent love affair, he had to admit, had made him jealous. He couldn't help but wonder what real girls were like and if they'd be as eager to put their arms around him in the Upperworld as they were in their dreams.

Hip hoped to soon have a taste of Jen's pretty lips. Maybe he'd get lucky and taste all of her.

Mrs. Holt looked at him now from behind the big stallion they called The General.

"You're as handy as your brother," Mrs. Holt said. "Too bad he couldn't come with you."

Jen stood up and brushed her mare's mane. "He's too busy with the wedding plans, I bet."

Hip couldn't stop the smile from crossing his face every time Jen looked at him through narrowed eyes. She recognized him, he was sure of it, but she was having trouble admitting to herself that she knew him from her dreams.

"I doubt that," Hip said with a shrug.

Jen whipped around to face him with her hands on her hips, her pretty mouth making a perfect "O." Then she said, "He better not make her do everything by herself. Damn your brother if he does."

This tickled Hip beyond control, and he couldn't stop himself from busting out laughing. What mortal had the gall to damn the god of death? Of course, this girl had no idea what she was saying.

"Language," Mrs. Holt said from the back of the barn.

Jen ignored her mother. "What's so funny?' She moved closer, her brown eyes glaring up at Hip from beneath her pretty blonde bangs and equally blond lashes. "Don't tell me you're a chauvinistic pig."

"Jen!" Mrs. Holt scolded from behind her beast. "Don't talk to Hip like that."

Jen kept her eyes blazing on Hip, but spoke to her mother. "I have the right to talk like that to anyone who laughs at me, Mama."

"My apologies," Hip said, reining in his chuckles. "But you misunderstood. Than's not busy with the wedding because, last I heard, Therese called it off."

Jen's mouth dropped open. Then, after staring incredulously at Hip for an uncomfortable amount of time, she threw her hands up in the air and presented him with a smile he hadn't earned. "Allelujah, praise the Lord! It's about time she came to her senses."

Was she praising *him*? Had he become her *lord*? Somehow he doubted it, but he was amused by how quickly Jen's demeanor changed from attack mode. She looked about to hug him. He liked being the bearer of good news.

"When's she coming home?" Jen asked him.

Hip shook his head. "I don't think she is. I, I…" He wished he'd kept his mouth shut. It wasn't his job to explain why a goddess couldn't live among her mortal friends and family.

Jen stepped between the horses and planted her feet inches from his. He wanted to reach out and touch her to see if she felt as good as she did in the Dreamworld. Her eyes narrowed and then widened, and for a moment, he thought she had figured out who he was. But then she said, "Don't tell me she's going to stay in Texas."

"Why would she…" Hip stopped himself. "Maybe you should talk to her yourself." He turned his back to her and continued to brush the horse. This conversation was over. He'd never had to make explanations to mortals, and he wasn't about to start doing it now.

But Jen moved close behind him, so close, he could feel the heat from her body. He could smell her sweat and something else. Something fruity and sweet.

"I can't get a hold of her," Jen said in a desperate voice. "She hasn't returned any of my texts and calls in over a month. I don't know if she has her new email yet. She's not on Facebook anymore, or Instagram. Nothing. It's like she's disappeared off the face of the earth."

She has, he wanted to say. That's exactly what's happened. But, of course, he wouldn't.

Jen put her hand on his shoulder and he felt every part of him come to attention.

"Please," she said softly. "Please help me get in touch with her."

He turned and saw tears welling in her eyes. "I'll do what I can."

***

Jen was surprised by the sudden tenderness in the new handler's voice. It reminded her of something from a dream. She closed her eyes and shook her head.

"What?" Hip asked, his face close.

She took a step back. "I need to get back to work."

As she brushed Satellite, Jen stole glances at Hip. He'd taken her out to a movie over a year ago when his brother had introduced them, but then he'd never called her again after that. He'd said he'd never been to this part of the world, as though he were from another country. But he was from Texas. He spoke as if Texas were in a different part of the world.

Well, maybe all Texans thought that way.

Now he had the gall to show his face and ask for a job. He could have called her just to say, "Hey."

She glanced at him once more, and this time she noticed a look of worry come over his face, even horror.

"You alright?" she asked. He was freaking her out.

He turned to Jen's mother and said, "I'm sorry, Mrs. Holt, but I have to go."

"What is it?" Jen's mom asked, also noticing the obvious look of horror on their new handler's face.

"I can't explain," he said. "Something's not right. I need to go immediately. My apologies."

"Do you need a ride anywhere?" Pete asked, having just walked in from the pen and having overheard the last bit of their conversation.

"Um, no thanks," Hip said. "Thanks anyway, man."

238

Jen's mouth dropped open. This made absolutely no sense. She followed Hip from the barn and stood at the gate, where he let himself out of the pen.

"Are you coming back tomorrow?" she asked.

"I don't know. I hope so." He didn't even look at Jen, which hurt after the tenderness between them moments ago. She'd begun to forgive him. And now he was leaving?

"Will I ever see you again?" she cried out as he jogged down the gravel drive from her house to the road.

"I hope so," he repeated, but again without turning and meeting her eyes.

Overcome with a sudden feeling of dread, Jen opened the gate and followed him down the path. She watched him turn past a line of oak trees. When she rounded the corner, her throat pinched closed by the shock. He had disappeared.

She looked all around the one-mile stretch of road from her house to the Melner Cabin, where he was staying. Panting for breath and trembling, she knocked on the door of the cabin and got no answer.

"Hip? Are you there?" she called again and again, but the boy had vanished.

***

To learn more about Eva Pohler's books, please visit her website at http://www.evapohler.com.

Made in the USA
Columbia, SC
02 August 2019